BRETHREN

First Edition

Andrew McDiarmid

Brethren

First Edition

Published by The Nazca Plains Corporation
Las Vegas, Nevada
2007

ISBN: 978-1-887895-68-2

Published by

The Nazca Plains Corporation ®
4640 Paradise Rd, Suite 141
Las Vegas NV 89109-8000

PUBLISHER'S NOTE
Brethren is a work of fiction created wholly by *Andrew McDiarmid's*
imagination. All characters are fictional and any resemblance to any
persons living or deceased is purely by accident. No portion of this
book reflects any real person or events.

Cover, Fleshblack Images
Art Director, Blake Stephens

FOREWORD

This has been a good journey to writing "BRETHREN". I have found a wonderful writing team in Matt, Eric, Doil, Cecil, Steve, and a certain cigarleatherman and his boy on the east coast. These men and women are my Brethren in many ways. They help me embrace worlds inside me that very few actually get to see. They allow me to open myself to them and allow the creative process to flow through me, and with their guidance, flourish. Without them, my writing would be good, but not excellent. I have often seen writers talk about writing groups in their books. Now I understand all too well their use and the comraderie one can find in them.There is of course the necessary thank you's for this project's completion:

For Tim Brough, ...your a good man...Mr. Brough.

For Matt Prather, I promise to return to the Brethren soon and explore them further

For Cecil, Eric, and Doil, for the people who are on the edge of this world i have created. Your new voices have created some new characters and new challenges.

For my Mum, who will never read this book but has been supportive of it from the day i started.

And for my twin brother, Robert, with whom i celebrate a 40th birthday when this book is released. There could be no one closer to my heart and i love you.

CONTENTS

BRETHREN
CHAPTER ONE

The biker stood in the middle of the smoke-filled room, unable to clarify his thoughts. Smoke would do that to him. He also acknowledged that this wasn't ordinary smoke. This was a special grey smoke that had only one source: the man sitting in the large chair, directly in front of the mesmerized biker. The large cigar held between his teeth reached out into the room with its scent. A large plume of smoke escaped through the thick moustache of the MASTER. With every release of smoke, the room became a fog of cigar smoke, and the scent of sweat that only the biker's MASTER could create.

There was one person whose eyes could burn through the thickest of fog, or the darkest of tobacco smoke. The biker could feel the smoke massaging him, almost as if it were guided to penetrate all of his senses. MASTER knew how to make him submit every time.

"You have spent many years in my service, and you have pleased me without fail. There are even a few of us who would say that your service to the Brethren has been 'exemplary.' But, we all understand that there is only one opinion that matters, don't we?" the man in the chair said in a soft tone.

"Yes, Master. There is no fault in your words, SIR," the biker answered.

The smoke seemed to lead him to his knees. Not that he was resisting, because kneeling before his Master was something he had done for over 200 years. Mack, as the biker had come to be known in modern times, had been this man's bodyguard and his sexual servant for far too long to resist the smoke. Mack's Master was in a very aggressive mood, and was being very ritualistic since Mack had returned from his patrol of the region.

The aroused state of his Master wasn't lost on the biker, either. A large uncut cock and the now familiar silver ring within it stared him down; the glisten of precum dripping off the foreskin, taunting him.

"Ah, there will be time for feeding on your Master's flesh—and oh yes, you will feed…"

The biker found himself drooling at the thought.

"My dear hungry slave, there are many things coming that neither of us can control. We are entering an age of man, where hiding as well as we have will be coming to an end. Even in the wilderness we call home."

The biker then began to remove his chaps.

"Yes, slave, wondered when you would remember to remove your garments as I speak to you. Maybe the years of service lag your memory of protocol?"

The biker felt the caress of the smoke as his jacket was removed. The grey fog seemed to reach to his chest, teasing his nipples, arousing his whole body.

"We also must look to the future, when I am no longer here."

The biker flinched. The smoke slid into to his open mouth and forced its way into his lungs. For a brief moment, he couldn't breathe. The man in the chair then leaned forward and took in a deep breath of air. The smoke seemed to release itself from the biker, and pour itself into the man in the chair.

"Listen now, there will be time to talk later. Do as you're told, and focus on my words."

The man let out a deep breath of smoke, and it resettled itself around the biker. The words were pouring into the biker's mind as the smoke continued its massage.

The man in the chair smiled as he continued to speak.

"There is a foreigner coming to our lands. I have not been given the identity of this stranger, just that he is coming, and he is to serve you—and therefore, serve me."

The biker saw the smoke rise between them, forming a face. Staring at the face in the smoke, the biker felt a hunger he had not felt before, domination pouring out of him. The man in the chair smiled.

"The stranger is coming, and we have much to prepare, for the stranger is human."

The biker gasped, even knowing the consequences. The MASTER took in another long drag on his cigar. He let out the long stream of smoke that wrapped around them both. The smoke again attacked his lungs, this time not releasing so quickly, but leaving the biker completely under the other man's control.

"Oh yes, the same submission you feed to me, the human will feed to you…" growled the Master, stepping out of the chair.

The smoke released from the biker's lungs and returned to its Master.

"Are you ready for more smoke?" the man asked.

The biker always liked the way Master asked the question, although the answer was always the same.

"Yes, MASTER."

The foreskin slowly pulled away from the piercing, and precum began to drip down the ringed metal. The Master's cigar came back to life. The ember grew dark red with the deep inhale of the Master. There was hint of love and respect from the Master's eyes as a single drop of precum splashed onto the floor.

"Now, slave, submit to my smoke!"

Smoke poured from the Master's lungs in huge, grey, woody gushes. The smoke poured down over the biker, and there was a great pressure over his entire body. His Master then brought his dripping cock to the biker's beard.

"Feed, my slave!"

The smoke and flesh invaded the biker's throat and there was no other thought available other than "Yes, MASTER!"

PRAIRIE, KANSAS
Hwy. 70, Exit 47

Sometimes there is no one hearing the cursing that pours out when your car breaks down. It was one of those moments that people would laugh over later, but now the only thing going through Gregory's mind was "FUCK ME." The bad type of "fuck me".

The late afternoon sun had been beating down on the 35-year-old man and his blue station wagon for over an hour now. Parts of his transmission still glistened in the relentless summer heat. He had looked at the map, and it was a good two miles each way to an exit. He had no water except for the now toasty warm diet soda in the front seat of his car. The rest of the car was filled with his belongings. Gregory was moving to Texas.

Leave it to him to break down in the middle of Dorothy country on the Friday night of Memorial Day Weekend. It was just his luck.

The decision to move to Texas had been marred by several problems right from the get go. His apartment building wouldn't let him out of his lease, although he had been laid off and out of work for three months. Work just wasn't finding him. There were times that the B.A. in English just didn't seem to be getting him places quite like his father said it would. A bachelor's degree wouldn't make a tow truck magically appear.

He had cashed in his savings and put his entire life into the back of the station wagon. And now that all of his savings seemed to be spread out over three lanes of freeway, the future looked bleak.

It was at that moment that the flash of a windshield caught his eye.

Okay, maybe thinking of a tow truck was a good thing.

The large black tow truck came up behind his car and Gregory sighed, "Oh thank God."

Out from behind the wheel stepped a mountain of a man.

"You seem to be having car trouble…"

Gregory wanted to yell out…"Well duh! You think?!" but realized that probably would end up with him left alongside the highway, being told there wouldn't be another tow truck for hours.

"Well let's get that wagon hitched up and get you out of the heat. Prairie has a service station…looks like you might have major damage," the tow truck driver said.

"Sure—it's a step in the right direction."

Moments later Gregory found himself driving down the highway, with everything he owned bouncing behind him attached to the tow truck with a few rusty cables.

"Glad I made a run there, man. Looks like I got you just in time. There's some cold water in the cooler."

Gregory leapt with a thirst that was a little too obvious.

"Drink it slowly; don't want you passing out in my cab."

Two phone calls, insurance information, and one AAA card later, the station wagon was parked in front of Prairie Kansas GMC, which was closed for the holiday weekend. Four motels, a Burger King, a Dairy Queen, and miles and miles of plowed fields were all that greeted him.

"We'll lock your car in the garage till Tuesday…"

What choice did Gregory have, after all? He went into the wagon and pulled out enough clothes to cover a weekend and several books to read. He slipped them into a small suitcase. Soon he found himself waving goodbye to the tow truck driver and standing in front of one of the motels along the freeway.

He stepped into the entrance, and found a perky female at the counter.

Maybe if he went to sleep he could forget about being stuck in the middle of nowhere with a minimum of four days for repairs. They went through the pleasantries of "checking in."

"So where does one find dinner here?" he asked softly.

The woman behind the counter smiled.

"Well, young man like you has lots of choices: there is a lot of fast food restaurants on the other side of the freeway. and there is the bar as well. A lot of truckers go there," she said politely.

"Thank you then, room 5, right?

"Yes, Mr Carter, Room 5."

Gregory thanked her, slid his credit card back into his wallet and re-entered the summer heat. All of his belongings were in the station wagon back at the garage. He didn't look forward to spending several days in the small town, but it was the hand that was dealt.

He wandered down the side of the hotel. The warm fields of Kansas were at full bloom in summer. The forecast had been for temperatures well over 90. That was why he had decided to start out so early. He hoped that God would forgive him for the massive amounts of swearing when the car came to a grinding halt after crossing the Kansas border. He had drifted off the freeway at the first town, with the car gasping for air and lurching forward.

He came to the end of the building where he thought the young lady told him room #5 was. Something was reflecting the sun's brightness right in his way. As he moved further along the building, the reflection subsided to reveal its source. It was a heavily chromed motorcycle and it was parked directly in front of room #5.

Gregory walked to the door and slid his key in the door. Part of him was still admiring the motorcycle, as the door slid away from him. The door was suddenly opened by a very muscular man, half dressed.

"What the fuck?" he said loudly.

"The gal at the counter gave me this key, said my room was #5." Gregory answered softly.

"Well, I'm in number 5, the broad gave you the wrong key, boy."

Hearing the tall muscular man say "boy," made Gregory shiver. He figured that showing such emotion in the middle of Kansas was probably a good way to get killed.

"I'll go back and get the right key, sorry for disturbing you,"

Gregory continued.

"Do that, boy," said the man.

For a moment, Gregory thought he had seen a familiar reaction in the man's eyes. There were miles of dirt in his beard and face. The chest was covered in sweat and grime that riding across the country would give a man. Grey ash was smeared over his chest hair.

It was several moments until Gregory realized that the door was back in place, and the man had closed it. He walked back to the counter and told the woman the error. She apologized for her error and gave him the key to room 6. He once again entered the heat of the day. Room 6 finally greeted him. As he slid the key in the door, he turned back to the motorcycle parked in the lot. He wondered what adventures that bike had seen, and where its owner had taken it.

"Hey boy," a voice came softly.

Gregory momentarily didn't hear the soft voice.

"Boy!" the voice came louder.

The man in room 5 was now back at the door. The grime was replaced by finely combed, shoulder length grey hair resting on muscular shoulders that were still wet from a shower.

"Hello. Sorry, the sun must be getting to me. Sorry for the mix up," Gregory answered.

"I just wanted to say sorry, I don't like ripping into a guy like that. You just startled me," the man answered.

"It's okay...don't blame you for reacting that way, you never know who might be in these side freeway hotels..."

"How long you here for, boy?"

There he was using that term again. The biker was working Gregory's last nerve.

"Well, my car broke down, have to wait at least until Tuesday to get parts," Gregory said while shielding his eyes from the sun.

The man smiled.

"Well, there are worse places for a young man to be stuck," he said.

Gregory didn't necessarily agree with him.

"Well, I need to get in out of this heat—not used it—and take a shower."

The man seemed to look right through him. He couldn't explain it.

"Well, I am here on business for the next couple of days. Let me make it up to you by getting you a beer later."

Gregory didn't really remember agreeing to the biker's request, but regardless of how uncomfortable he was, he said yes to the biker's offer. He remembered how wonderful the shower was, how cool the hotel room was after the air conditioning started working, and how soft the bed was. Sleep took over any other thoughts.

Gregory woke several hours later and rolled over to look at the clock. It read 3:45. He walked to the window and looked out on to the flat prairie that was Kansas. The motorcycle that had so enthralled him was gone. The memory of the man who rode it made Gregory harden. While he was pretty sure that the man riding the bike probably had a wife at home (wherever that was), he was also pretty sure the biker had no plans on feeding that furry strong body to him. The body of the biker was enough to jack off to, dreaming about something that was probably better left to dreams.

Gregory lay across his bed and stroked to the thoughts of sexually pleasing his neighbor in the small hotel. The energy expelled in release dropped him back into sleep, and in his slumber he did not hear the motorcycle return. He did not see the man rise off the machine and smile towards his window, while adjusting his crotch.

"Yep, that boy will do very nicely," the man said softly in the wind.

The wind rustled round him, almost answering him with a "yesssssssssssssss" on the fields behind the hotel. The biker stared off at the distant home on the horizon and smiled brightly. Gregory never saw the man peering through the break in the curtain at his naked, revealed body. A gentle but aggressive smile pierced the beard of the older man.

"Yes, he'll do just fine."

The dim light outside woke Gregory about 6pm. He hated the fact that it never got dark till late in the summer. He much preferred the night, and he got less and less of it. June in Kansas was just relentless heat.

He slipped his jean shorts back on, as there was a knock on his door. Not worrying about putting a shirt on he went to the door. Standing on the other side was the owner of the Harley. He was dressed in one of those butch Harley shirts, with a couple of tears in it, a very worn pair of jeans, and tattered engineer boots. Gregory smiled.

"Evening. Sorry, I completely forgot about the offer for a beer, come on in while I get better dressed," Gregory said backing away.

He didn't get to see the cycle man grin at the view of his ass in the tight Levi shorts.

"One might recommend pants. Wearing shorts like that where we are going would not be such a good idea," the biker replied.

Gregory grabbed a pair of jeans from his suitcase and headed for the bathroom.

"I'll be right out," Gregory said to the biker.

The biker came fully into the room and closed the door. He sat in the chair by the window as Gregory headed for the bathroom.

"Fuck boy..." The biker muttered under his breath too low for Gregory to hear.

Gregory went behind the bathroom door. When the boy came out of the bathroom door in the jeans he found the biker had undressed, and now sat on the bed buck naked with a raging hardon between his legs. The uncut sleeve wrapped around a biker slice of man meat that Gregory had never seen before. It was larger than any cock he had witnessed before.

"Suck my cock, boy..."

Gregory leapt forward between the two incredibly furry legs. The cock twitched as he approached and Gregory swallowed. The taste was beyond his imagination. There was the sweet taste of sweat on this man's cock. That taste like "I showered, but I just let the water rinse here; I didn't use soap here".

The biker's hands were covered in skintight leather gloves. They grasped the back of Gregory's head and the man grunted.

"I said *suck* my cock, not *lick* it, boy!"

The biker forced his cock down the boy's throat. Gregory gagged. The biker didn't care. This boy was going to serve.

Gregory looked up from the biker's crotch.

"Are you ready?"

"Ready…"

As the alarm clock sounded, the biker vanished from the room, and Gregory opened his eyes. It was 5 p.m. His cock was hard between his legs, and the biker was nowhere to be seen. He would need a nice cold shower.

The road had always been the biker's friend. It was where he went to think and to remember the past. The young human had his cock thinking rough invasive sex. His emotions poured out of him, and the road became a warm comfort as the motorcycle sped across the blacktop.

The biker found himself already fantasizing Master's smoke enveloping the two of them, and the new slave feasting on his new Master's cock, as the biker's cock violated his ass, claiming it as his, all the while the smoke caressing the three of them into a union.

Master had been quite clear. The boy would have to choose the union of his own free will, and that could take several days of intense interaction with the boy. The boy in room #6 had no idea what he found himself in. Prairie, Kansas would be his new home. He just didn't know it yet.

What was going to be the hardest to reveal was that Master was well over 900 years old, and that Mack himself, was 400 years old. They were Brethren. How to explain to a human who had a life expectancy of 70-80 years, that the biker had begun life in Europe and the tobacco trade led him to the "New World," where fantastic treasures awaited those who dared to travel there? How to tell the boy in the room down the hall how Mack had found himself on the mighty Mississippi River? Finding himself in a new world, after many brutal years in Europe. In Virginia, he found a man that would tug at his heart for many years.

For now Mack, let the road and roar of the engine let him remember things long since past. Remembering first coming to the United States, and finding his first taste of love with another Brethren.

1706, VIRGINIA

Master Wolf was not the first man, human or otherwise, with whom Mack had been intimate. In 1706, Mack was known as MacElroy Tanner. He came to the new world in search of a renewed life. He knew there was money in the new tobacco crop. MacElroy was a courier. He brought the payment from England, from the Brethren Tobacco Consortium. This voyage led him to a plantation in Virginia. After the laborious voyage across the Atlantic, MacElroy found himself traveling to the Shields plantation. It was something unlike anything he had seen before.

But in 1705, "Sapponckanican" were everywhere. That was what Indians called them. The tobacco fields as far as the eye could see, acres of tobacco and the ever-present slaves picking it and processing it for shipment. MacElroy wasn't quite sure why he was sent here. He knew that the person in charge of the production lived in the new world, but he wasn't in Virginia. Why did MacElroy have to find his way to this plantation?

The Shields Plantation was a very large facility. From the hills of the farm one could see the hundreds of slaves working in the fields. Ah, yes, owning another's man literal flesh was something commonplace. But this was not slavery on the terms on which Macelroy would eventually enter into. Willing slavery is an emotional bond and it is service to another without resistance. It is wanting to serve, instead of being forced to against one's will.

The older slaves could look up in his eyes and see something that the white men didn't ever seem to notice. Slaves knew what he was.

He was living a lie. He was not accustomed to seeing people who could see through that lie. But there are species of humans that pay attention more than most. Slaves were from a very powerful culture.

"Good morning, Master…" the low bass voice greeted.

MacElroy looked up from the road to find a tall, slender and muscular African American.

"I am no Master…" MacElroy replied sternly.

"You are, more than most, Massa, and as Master Shields' guest, you are a Master to this slave. Master Shields is expecting you."

The traveler found himself drawn to the tall dark man in front of him, who stood 6 foot 3 and wore ragged clothes. The moment Mack made a connection with his greeter's eyes, he saw many years there.

"As said, Massa, Master Shields is expecting YOU," the slave said.

"But you are older than I?" MacElroy responded.

"But you's white."

"I am not familiar with the world here, it seems so different."

"Of course, there are many new ways here. Comes with the new territories i tells ya. we'll get you up to the house Now Master SIR… He's waiting for ya…"

The two men made their way through the fields. As the slave said nothing, MacElroy scanned several other older-than-they-appeared men out in the fields, working the tobacco. There was a reason that this plantation was doing well. It had an inside track. Shields didn't just have slaves, he had slaves that had been alive for several hundred years. Tobacco was just another crop to them. MacElroy never quite understood why the Brethren amongst slaves didn't try to be more than they were.

The slave that had met him at the ship had put it quite quaintly.

"We ain't no fools, Massa MacElroy…Just cause we are different than the other men, don't mean that the white man's gun couldn't kill us just the same. Just cause my father was round when Jesus was alive don't mean I get no fair shake. I'm in this with my human brothers. Bein' owned is bein' owned!" the slave had explained.

MacElroy was relieved, however, that the slaves upon Shields' farm were taken care of. The slave quarters stood at the top of the fields, and the Master's house stood with brilliant brick and warm coziness. The familiar glint in the man's eyes almost gave him a humbling feel.

"Ah, Dade…I see you found Master MacElroy," a Southern voice drawled.

The traveler turned to the front steps of the plantation house, and found a very striking figure. He stood well over 6 feet, just shy of 200 pounds, with a large thick moustache covering his face and a large cigar clenched in his teeth.

"Welcome to Virginia, Master MacElroy. I'm Shields."

"Good Evening, Master Shields,"

Shields turned to the slave and bowed his head.

"Leave us…"

Shields smiled as he turned his attention back to the new arrival. The slave returned to the fields, and left the traveler outlined in the afternoon sun.

"You must be parched after that walk up from town?" Shields questioned.

MacElroy was still distracted by the handsome features of his host.

"As always, Wolf has chosen well, you'll be a welcome addition to his household. But he's a good three week ride from here, and you ain't fitted for that journey yet. Get in the house and out of those heavy clothes."

MacElroy obeyed his host and stepped up on the porch. He slowed his pace as he got within the cloud of smoke that hovered around Shields.

"Lemonade first, smoke later—understand me?" Shields said sternly.

"Yes, SIR!"

"Good Lad. We don't get many of your kind here… I got a lot of seed release to be producing later, and you better be ready."

"Yes, SIR!"

MacElroy stepped into the house and removed his overcoat as Shields instructed. He turned to find the older man with a large grin on his face.

"You need a good wash. I think you'll enjoy the way we take

baths here on my plantation."

MacElroy didn't know whether to trust that smile or fear it. He continued to remove his heavy garments and enjoyed feeling the breeze brush against his skin. Shields stepped forward with his cigar now releasing smoke like a burning chimney. The scent was unmistakable. There was something about Brethren Tobacco that gave it a unique scent.

"Yeah, made sure I had some of Wolf's blend waitin' for ya."

MacElroy found it hard to speak.

"Don't worry. You don't need to talk where I'm taking ya."

Shields started towards the back of the house, and let his coat drop to the ground, revealing a tightly woven strand of hair down his back. Hints of grey looped through the dark black hair.

"Come on, pup...time to wash up, and get to know each other better."

The memories dropped behind the biker as he opened the throttle full wide on the bike. He rode through the hills outside the small town in Kansas unable to control the raging hard cock between his legs. The old man could still affect him like that, even in daydreams. But then again, Shields always could. Mack found the historical marker alongside the 2-lane highway and parked his bike. He walked into the golden field as he took out his cock and began stroking hard. The leather glove was working up an orgasm quite efficiently.

He walked towards the small grove of oak trees in the center of the field.

"You could always make me react quickly..." The biker said to the wind.

Not holding back at all, the biker released a load of cum over the ground, and then wiped his brow with the cum-covered glove. The sweat on his brow mixed with the cum and leather to allow that unique scent fill the air.

"It's my turn now Master Shields. I hope he meets your approval..."

With that simple statement, Mack turned back around to his bike. Back in the grove of trees, there was a significantly larger tree in the center. Carefully carved into the back was a simple sentence. "For Shields, 1867."

The biker brought his motorcycle back to life, and turned back towards town. He had appointments to keep.

CHAPTER TWO

Gregory stood in the rain unable to understand the emotions that were swirling around him. The deck of the house that he had built with his partner of many years just didn't seem to matter any more. After the funeral, he had stood naked in the rain crying. It was the only emotion left for him. On the deck was the letter slowly fading in the rainwater. The darkness of the spring night slowly took Gregory and the rain into its embrace. Standing in the spring rain would land him in bed for several days with a horrible cold. He also found, while lying in bed for three days coughing and sniffling, that he began to assess his life. Was Denver where he belonged? or was there something more just over the horizon?

In the months leading up to summer, he sold everything in the house through garage sales, put the house up for sale, and decided to leave Denver behind. His company gave him the transfer to Dallas, and while it wasn't exactly a promotion, there was a new future waiting for him in Texas. Although in hindsight, he should not have chosen to travel to Texas in the middle of summer.

And now he found himself crying in the shower of a motel in podunk Kansas with a shattered transmission. It was just the last straw. Now he was going to spend his savings on fixing the car, and the hotel room. He turned the water off, and slowly toweled himself off. Gregory was actually hoping that the biker would show up. How weird was it that the biker had offered him a beer? Having a beer with a straight biker in the middle of Kansas was pretty much right up there with the other "new things" he had experienced since deciding to leave Denver behind.

But Gregory found himself thinking of the biker, in spite of himself. Not really like his ex-lover, though the age was about right. The biker was in his forties, and that was the age range the boy normally fell for. He found himself thinking all the wrong thoughts as his toweled off his hair and put on his jeans. Tennis shoes, and a blank green t-shirt, the plain look.

Mack knocked on the boy's door about 5:30 p.m. A nice firm knock. The biker blinked his eyes and the young man from this afternoon was now standing in front of him in jeans, a blank green T-shirt and cowboy boots.

"My name is Gregory," the young man said.

"Nice meeting you, Gregory. People call me Mack."

There was a slight accent in the biker's voice. It aroused the boy.

They shook hands. The boy was nervous, and Mack liked it. Gregory was trembling in front of him. Boys that trembled were normally the ones that were holding back. There was plenty of time to relax this boy and allow him to show his true nature. Modern people just didn't take the time to take in the scent of humans. From the fresh-showered scent the biker could tell so much more. Mack just knew this was not only a good homosexual submissive but one that, if trained properly, would find a good place in the clan---and most of all, one that Master Wolf would approve of. But, he was getting ahead of himself.

"You hungry, Gregory?" Mack asked.

"A little, i just woke up from a nap, i haven't eaten yet this afternoon."

Damn, the boy had a wonderful use of the English language. His English was impeccable. He had probably done very well in school and had a quality upbringing.

"Hungry…" Mack muttered.

Gregory turned to the biker with a questioning look.

"Sorry, didn't catch that?"

Fuck. Mack had to get his act together. Part of him wanted to just shove this boy against the wall in the back of the hotel and shove his cock deep inside him turning him into a slave in one swift set of thrust fucks. But there were rules. Assessments had to be made. Mack had to be sure before luring the boy into things he could only imagine.

Others had rushed the process, only to have failures. He wasn't going to be part of that group of men, who remained in the corners of the mist and smoke, with an empty collar and empty heart.

"So you want to catch dinner and a beer then? We could combine them..." Gregory said.

"That sounds like a plan, but I'm only buying you the beer," Mack said confidently.

"No problems. Guess it is just nice to have company out here."

"Kansas isn't as bad as you might think once you get to know it. Even Oklahoma and Nebraska could have many things to offer you," Mack answered.

"Well, I am heading to Texas, actually. If they can ever get my car going."

Mack smiled as he led the boy through simple conversation, and distracted the boy from noticing that the road stop coffee shop they were walking up to hadn't been there when the boy arrived in Prairie, Kansas. They walked through the door, and the smoke billowed out like fog. A very simple neon sign in dark blue read "Wolf's Café."

Behind the counter was a large man with a thick Fu Manchu moustache. He wore a simple uniform. Blue jeans, a plain short sleeve shirt, His name tag read "M. Wolf".

"Table for two?" the waiter asked.

"Yes, for two…?"

"Smoking or non-smoking…"

Gregory turned to Mack for the answer.

"Smoking, if you don't mind,"

"Smoking…"

M. Wolf led them into the smoky side of the restaurant.

"Here's a good booth. What will you all drink?"

"Coffee with cream for me," Mack said.

"And for the young man?" the waiter asked.

"Water is fine for now, thank you."

"Water and creamed coffee. Thank you; your server will be right with you."

Mack and Gregory sat down into the booth. Over half of the booths were filled with men talking and smoking. There were a couple of women at several of the tables.

"You can tell this is a popular trucker stop," Gregory said.

"How so?" Mack asked.

"All the men alone, or in small groups. Only in the trucker cafes do you see lots of men eating and few women."

There were other places, Mack knew that. Yes, a lot of men tended to have their meals at the roadstop, but it was for many other reasons than good food and service. The biker was aware that his Master was the owner of the establishment. The boy had no idea his future Master was quietly looking him over while asking what they wanted to drink. M. Wolf on the name tag for most meant Mr. Wolf, but to those who knew, it read MASTER WOLF.

"One water, and one coffee with cream," M. Wolf said quietly, interrupting Mack's thoughts.

Gregory didn't notice the wet stain on the waiter's pants, or the gentle smile given to Mack. There was nothing like the coffee at Wolf's Cafe, and the cream was half the reason for asking for coffee.

"Enjoy your meal, gentlemen," the waiter said and quietly walked away.

There were other customers to attend to, after all.

Gregory had been having a hard time focusing on the meal, and stopping his fantasies about the biker. The beer had been cold and the conversation had been simple enough.

Gregory and Mack finished their meal and talked about politics, and the way of the world. Gregory kept wondering where all this was supposed to be going. After all, he was probably a straight biker, and Gregory was a thirty-year-old gay man. Kinship probably was the last thing on the biker's mind.

"So tell me...Gregory... are you gay?" the biker asked as he drank the last mouthful of beer from his glass.

Gregory shifted in his seat, not really sure how to answer. The biker grinned as the beer left his mouth and slid down his throat.

"Don't worry boy, not asking you loudly, and don't expect a

loud answer. This isn't the place for a true discussion…if it makes you feel better... I am as well. Or does that surprise you?"

Gregory now really shifted in his seat.

"Well, yes. It does surprise me, to a point ."

Mack smiled.

"Don't worry, young man. There are many things about me I think you would like…"

Gregory smiled.

"Such as?" Gregory whispered.

"I think we need to return to the motel for that discussion. Let's enjoy our meal first," the biker answered, with a wide toothy grin.

The biker laughed.

"You have training in you. Most kids coming off the freeway from the big city don't know the first thing about treating a man with manners."

Inside Mack's thoughts continued, "I'm hoping you were trained right in other ways as well, boy." but outside it just produced a smile.

The waiter returned to the table.

"Mack, you know how we always appreciate your ability to lift heavy things, could I get your help in the back for a second?" M. Wolf asked.

"Sure thing, Wolf…"

Mack stood up, matching his tall frame alongside Master Wolf. The two men looked down at the quiet calm boy. Master Wolf could smell the arousal on both the biker and the boy. Restraint was in order, but Wolf knew that once he got a good taste of the biker and the boy together, holding back would never happen again.

"Wait right here for me, boy…understand?" Mack said softly but sternly.

"Yes, SIR." Gregory answered.

Gregory could feel his cock harden and a slight chill slip over his body as he answered the biker so honestly.

"Good boy. I thought we would get along fine. Now this is going to take me a second. Need to take care of something with the owner. Back in ten minutes, boy, then we'll take you back to the motel and see what else you are good at."

Gregory didn't answer this time, he just smiled.

"Good boy…" the biker said as he left the table.

Gregory was amazed that he called him "boy" in front of the waiter. The two hairy men standing before him were quite a sight. The one named Wolf had a full day's sweat upon his brow from working in the kitchen. The thick moustache was always something of a weakness for the boy. Facial hair was becoming a requirement for him to find a man handsome. A clean-shaven man would have to be quite handsome to catch his eye.

The two men walked away from the boy, leaving the fresh scent of man sweat lingering in the air.

The biker followed his MASTER back into the rooms behind the counter. They walked pensively through the kitchen. Wolf stopped briefly at the cook and smiled.

"Feed…"

Wolf raised up his arm and pulled back the shirt to reveal a dark brown sweaty armpit. The cook dove in with a ravenous licking, getting every drop of sweat. The MASTER lowered his arm, and tapped the top of the cook's head.

"That's a good servant, back to work now…"

Master Wolf continued on to an office. The biker followed Wolf through the kitchen to a small office. They walked in and the biker immediately knelt before his Master.

"The boy has promise, SIR," Mack said softly with his head bowed.

"Good. Show him the pleasure of my slave's flesh, and turn the boy to your pleasure. If he is to be your cub, you realize he will become my new slave, and you will now be one of the clan's leaders?"

"Yes Master, the slave now realizes your pleasure and mine," the biker said with his head bowed.

The waiter undid his pants, and pulled out his large uncut cock.

"Look up, MacElroy. Look at the arousal you are capable of, even in my office."

The biker obeyed and saw the cock thicken as they talked.

"You have served the clan without fail these many years. Now fate has brought you an excellent boy, and a new slave for my pleasures. The clan will also like him, I feel—although his facial hair will need to grow. But you know those rules well, don't you, slave?" the waiter asked.

"Yes, Master, I know your rules well. You trained this slave well."

The waiter smiled.

"You always had a way of making me want to reward you... Not that the boy sitting in booth four isn't reward enough—he has great potential. Drink your Master's piss, slave."

Mack licked his lips.

"Yes, Master, proudly!"

The biker wrapped his lips around his Master's cock and drank the warm salty fluid that started to flow.

"That's a good slave…drink it all... And then feed all I give to you to your boy out there."

The liquid gold slid down the biker's throat and his whole body felt warmer. He could feel the cock of his Master grow as the liquid slowly subsided and the uncut flesh slowly pulled out of his eager throat and mouth.

"My property has done well. Continue to do so."

"Yes, Master!"

"Dismissed…"

In the café Gregory sat in incredible anticipation. He never thought a man that looked like this biker would ever find a thin moustached thirty-something, with a slight furry gut, attractive. He had had some interaction with leathermen, but not like this. He had a feeling this biker was more than just one of the men in leather at the bar — much more, actually.

The biker returned with a gentle smile on his lips.

"Ready to order, pup?" the biker asked.

Gregory smiled at the name.

The two men settled into a simple meal of meatloaf and mashed potatoes. Several beers each and they were quite relaxed. The biker then paid the check and turned back to the boy.

"We are going back to my room, and we'll be there all night. You have any issues with that pup?"

"No, Sir!"

"Let's get a move on, then." the biker said.

The two men made their way to the front of the café, where M. Wolf was waiting for them.

"Hope everything was to your satisfaction?" the waiter asked.

"Very much, Sir, thank you," Gregory answered.

Gregory stared into the waiter's eyes and found a strange comfort in them, almost as if the waiter knew where they were going and what they would do. If he didn't know better, he'd think the waiter was smiling in the knowledge of what the biker was going to do to him in the hotel room.

"Have a good evening, young man." the waiter said, "And Mack, thank you for your continued help."

"Most welcome. We're off..."

The young man and the biker walked out the front door of the restaurant. The main chef from behind the counter came up to the waiter with a gracious smile.

"Is that the new slave cub, Master?" the chef asked.

"Yes, Daniel, he is," the waiter answered.

The chef smiled.

"There is hunger in the wind tonight, bear. When we close up, the others and I will clean up. You will go to my chambers and strip. My cock needs a warm place to sleep..."

The chef simply answered "Yes, Sir," and walked towards the door at the end of the counter. The waiter greeted the next group of men to enter the front door.

"Welcome to Wolf's... Smoking or non-smoking?" he said with smile.

Gregory walked out to the warm air of a summer night in Kansas and many thoughts filled his mind. The biker grabbed the boy's neck and took a firm hold. He could feel the boy jump in anticipation.

"Don't worry pup, I don't hurt a boy, especially during first exploration. I intend to find out your strengths, the things you do really well. But do know this: you will wake up with my cock pressed against you. What do you think of that?" the biker asked.

Gregory gasped.

"Don't know if there is a bad thing to say about that, actually," he answered.

In the window of the building behind them stood the figure of the waiter, the shirt undone, the "MP WOLF" nametag hanging loosely from the fabric, the sweat of the day collecting on his forehead. He watched his slave of the past years walk into the distance with the possible new flesh for his pleasure. It had been many years since a new slave had appeared that aroused him. Mack had found a good specimen of slave. He was also reassured that Mack was the perfect vehicle to bring this new young man to his family.

Gregory woke several hours later with the hard cock of the biker still firmly lodged against his ass. He had never met anyone that could shoot a load like that and still stay hard. The biker had still had a firm hold on him---and it felt right.

The biker had taken him back to the hotel and told him to strip. Room 5 became much smaller once he knelt before this biker who was now wearing his chaps and nothing else. So many magazines had tried to describe the feelings that went through Gregory's head right now, but they had all failed miserably. Gregory had felt almost in a sexual fog since the biker told him they were going to have sex.

"My cock is ready for you, boy."

Gregory moved forward.

"But, before you get that cock you should know I don't do one night stands. You and I are going to get to know each other, and explore leather s/m and slavery, pup."

The words made Gregory tingle inside.

"Yes, I said slavery. You like those words, boy?" the biker asked.

"Yes Sir!"

The boy could see precum sliding out of the tip of the biker's cock.

"You will get to know my body better than any other. And you will meet the others in my clan. Yes. We have a clan of men like you and me. I have a Master, who you will meet. You will meet my brothers. So you need to know: You swallow my cock, and you are mine. Period."

Gregory couldn't move.

"You want this, don't you, boy?" Mack asked.

"Yes, Sir, I do."

Mack moved forward, and stood up from the bed.

"Then raise up to my cock, boy, and feast like you have never feasted!"

The salty precum met his lips and Gregory felt the warm embrace of the biker's hands. It was where he had dreamed of being. Not just from the bike being outside less than 24 hours ago, but for many years. The leather community had supplied him with knowledge and so many urges, but he had never found the right person. Could this be the right person? Gregory didn't know. But damn, the man opened so many pleasures already.

Gregory went to try and move out of the bikers grip those several hours later, but the biker held onto him; the grip and the man cock pressed against him left him awake and aroused. The gentle pressing of the cock against his ass eventually became a beckoning rhythm. He would find himself begging to be fucked by this man. But the biker said fucking comes to a boy who earns it. The rhythm finally rocked into an aroused slumber.

Gregory's last thought before sleep was that if he was to be broken down in the middle of Kansas with a weekend of waiting for parts and several more days of repairs, there was no better way to spend it. This biker had shown up by accident and had taken him where no man had in a long time. He partially feared that. The biker had more places to take him. The biker had a group—a clan, he said.

Morning would give Gregory time to ask more about that. He tightened his grip around the biker's arm and went back to sleep. Sleep allowed the past to creep back into his subconcious.

1706

Shields had filled the room with big clouds of smoke. They stood naked with each other in the large pool of warmed water. This was not where MacElroy had expected to be on his voyage to the new world. Shields had been going through standard conversation as the warm water soothed their bodies.

"Master Shields, I wanted to thank you for the tobacco use. It is quite a wonderful scent."

Shields smiled.

"Oh, but you haven't yet experienced the true pleasure of this scent. Not by a long shot, my young friend."

MacElroy looked confused.

"You are of the Brethren that beds with men, are you not?"

MacElroy seemed to flush.

"You wouldn't have been brought to a farm of someone who didn't share this inclination with you, young one. You have been on a long journey across the ocean. You need release."

The traveler again found himself unable speak as the water seemed to warm around him.

"The time for small talk is over, young one…"

Shields rose out of the water revealing a full erect manhood easily 9 inches long. It was a weapon. The older man slowly fed the younger man his cock. There was a sweetness in the manflesh that MacElroy hadn't tasted in many months.

"That's it, my boy. Do what comes naturally."

Soon, MacElroy left thought to the wind and consumed the cock sliding down his throat. The manly grasp of the back of his head, and the rising of energy between the two beings was warming the whole room.

"That's it, feed…"

The warmth in the room continued to build.

"Draw it out, young one. You need it, then it's my turn."

The cigar smoke from the plantation owner poured down over them and mingled from the steaming mist of the bath. It was an intense sensation for the young Brethren as the Master fed him his cock. The thick stream of manseed poured down his throat. It was a nourishing feeding indeed. Shields then lifted the younger brethren out of the water.

"now, its my turn…

Shields put the naked boy over his shoulder and carried him into the next room. A large bed greeted them, and Shields dropped the handsome young lad upon it. Shields then dropped to his knees and took MacElroy's cock in his throat. Saliva poured in around MacElroy's cock. The two men knew there was three months of pent up energy held deep inside.

Shields pulled away, briefly.

"That's a good boy, give me what I want."

MacElroy couldnt resist the expert oral skills of the elder who was quite efficiently emptying his balls.

"I can't hold back…" MacElroy proclaimed.

"Never asked you to, now did I?" Shields answered.

With a great roar MacElroy released his energy down the throat of the elder. It came in torrents and buckets. The elder swallowed greedily as some of the seed poured down the edges of his mouth and into his beard and moustache.

Shields had not experienced such release in many years. He continued to gulp and grasp at every drop of the seed and energy pouring out of the young Brethren laying before him.

Shields looked up with a wide smile.

"Good man. Welcome to my corner of the world." Shields said with a continuing smile.

Shields slid up to the bed and laid against the young man.

"Thank you, Sir." MacElroy whispered.

"Oh, most welcome," Shields said with a wide smile, "I have so much to teach you."

CHAPTER THREE
PRESENT

"I have so much to teach you," Mack said to the boy.

It was the first rule of riding on the motorcycle. The boy would have his arms around Mack, every time, holding onto him, and not the cycle. They found themselves flying down the 2-lane highway burning into the prairie that was Kansas. Gregory had learned how to hold on to the man doing the driving. It was not an easy lesson.

"You hold on to me, not the bike. You move with me, not the bike," Mack had instructed.

Gregory had slowly come to understand the rules. He paid attention to the biker at all times. It wasn't hard to do. The throat fucking he had received the previous night really put him to work. He knew he would be pleasing this man in all things, to find himself back between those legs. They were driving north. Mack had said there were several errands that they had to attend to that were to the north.

The boy had reveled in watching the landscape fly. It was a new experience. He was really amazed how short a period it was between grabbing onto the biker for dear life, and truly enjoying being a passenger.

Lunch had come in the form of luncheon meat on bread that was slightly squashed in the storage bin on the motorcycle. Two root beers that fizzed all over the grass from the short trip from the A&P to the rest area on the freeway, and honey buns were the remainders of the meal. Gregory however was still slightly dazed from his morning ventures on the motorcycle, going down the road at over 55 miles per hour, buzzing along the pavement. The wind had blown through his buzzed hair as he held on for dear life to the biker that took him out on the highway. After a while he had relaxed a bit, letting Mack breathe normally.

They spoke of many things that afternoon and morning. Mack had said that since they had the weekend to spend together, and his car wouldn't be ready till at least Wednesday that they could fly out into the expanse of Kansas. The effect of the highway flying under his feet made Gregory forget about all his troubles. Mack always seemed to know how to arouse Gregory. The biker knew where to touch, where to rub, to keep Gregory aroused.

"Well, I need to take a piss, and you are coming with me boy," the biker said

Gregory delayed for a moment, but there was something in the biker's voice that made it clear that coming with him to the bathroom wasn't a request; Gregory was being told what to do. Part of Gregory resisted, but the booming voice of the biker's order aroused him more than he was comfortable with.

They reached the middle section of the rest area. There was only one car in the car side of the area with an older couple just sitting down into their car. They were departing. In the truck area was a large 16-wheel truck with a gray flame along its side. Inset on the flame was a single word: "Wolf".

Gregory followed the biker into the men's room and the scent of old piss and rust filled his nostrils. He kept waiting for the biker to stop as they passed the standing urinals and they began to pass the stalls. The handicap stall was at the end with the door slightly ajar. The biker walked in. Gregory stalled. The biker came back to the edge of the door, and said simply, "Get on in here, boy, we can't start without you."

The boy came around the edge of the stall door to find a large muscular man sitting on the toilet with a raging hard on. He had a dark black beard that reminded him of the type that rock bands had: long and full. There was a tattoo on his arm that reached from his right wrist up the arm and leapt over to his back... Two very distinct sets of claw marks tattooed into his skin, and within the marks a set of searing eyes. Dark red, inviting, yet witha sense of danger. Gregory started to back out.

44

The tattooed man then smiled.

"Where the fuck do you think you're going. Get the fuck in here and lock that door!" he said in a tone that made Mack's pale in comparison.

Gregory moved forward, then noticed that Mack now had his commanding cock out, stroking it and looking at Gregory. Then Gregory noticed another small man knelt in the corner, covered in piss. The man couldn't have been more than 5' 5", a small compact man covered in fur, almost like a carpet. But for now the carpet was drenched in what appeared to be a fresh coat of piss.

"Yeah, my cub likes to be drenched in piss. You'll come to like it as well," the tattooed man said.

Mack turned to Gregory.

"Show the man the proper respect," Mack said to him.

Gregory moved forward not really knowing how to respond.

"Kneel, boy," the tattooed man commanded.

His voice seemed to console Gregory, as he dropped to his knees. Mack smiled. Then something happened that not even 48 hours ago would have offended Gregory deeply. From the head of the hard cock of the tattooed man came a steady stream of piss, pouring over Gregory's chest.

"That's it, boy, wear my piss."

The boy then felt the second stream of piss, this one coming from Mack. Not only was the biker pissing on him, his cock was coming closer and closer, splashing piss on Gregory's hair, and down his back.

"Swallow his cock," Mack commanded. "Yes, I know it's still pissing, guess you are going to have to drink it."

Gregory stalled again.

"Don't make me ask twice, boy," Mack said.

Gregory moved forward and the stream of piss came to his mouth, as a smile slid across the beard of the tattooed man. The piss didn't bother Gregory nearly as much; it just tasted like salty water. He began to swallow and the hard cock reached inside his mouth. A large leather glove came to the back of his head, and the tattooed man's smile widened.

The thirst growing in Gregory was intense. He had never wanted something so badly. He needed this man's piss.

Gregory continued to drink, forgetting about Mack for the moment and focusing on the fat uncut cock draining into his mouth. If he had stood around, he would see Mack feeding the piss covered cub his piss and cock, the cub drinking hungrily and that glassy stare falling over Mack's eyes. But it was the growing cock in his throat that kept his attention. The tattooed bear seemed to like his abilities, as the cock continued to throb, 'til the piss dribbled to a stop.

"Now suck that cock boy, like a good boy should!"

The four men plowed into the darkness of bliss. Two cocks filling two warm pliable holes, and two willing souls to fill. It went on for what Gregory thought was hours, the tattooed bear's cock filled his throat well, when suddenly the tattooed man pulled back out of his throat, with Gregory almost moving forward to get it back again.

"There will be plenty of time for this to continue. You are bringing the boy to the cabin, aren't you, Mack?"

Gregory still sat in a daze.

"I haven't asked the boy. You wish to come with your Daddy and his buddy —and of course piss pig here," as he pointed to the cub, "to the bonfire?"

Deep inside, Gregory knew the only way to answer. He took the biker's cock into his mouth. Mack smiled at the boy and looked pleased.

"Yes, I think the boy and I will be at the bonfire,"

Mack started plowing, Gregory's attentions quickly brought back to his Daddy Biker. Gregory could feel Mack's balls start to tighten and then in a roar like he had only heard from the biker, a fresh load of cum poured past his tongue to his gut.

Mack told the boy to stand, zip himself up and head for the door. The piss cub crawled across the floor to his tattooed bear's cock. He looked up slightly at Gregory and there was great pride in his eyes.

"Suck..." the tattooed man said.

The cub then dropped his focus to his Master's cock. Gregory and Mack could hear the massive slurping all the way out of the bathroom.

Just as the door opened to reveal the daylight to their eyes, there was an unmistakable... roar of a man losing his load down another's throat.

"The bonfire will be something that you will enjoy."

Gregory winced.

"What is a bonfire, Sir?"

"Well a bunch of truckers, bikers, and uninhibited pigs—who also just happen to enjoy the company of other men, or whats that new term...gay—meet out at Wolf's property for a bonfire and evening of barbeque and sexual freedom," Mack answered.

"Sounds inviting…"

"You'll never be the same afterward, once the clan has met you."

"The clan? You have used that term before?" Gregory asked.

"The wolf clan. Master Wolf's clan."

Mack could see the outline of a rock hard cock in his boy's piss soaked jeans. They walked over to the bike, and smiled to each other as a family in station wagon pulled by, with the wife showing astonishment for Gregory's piss soaked pants.

"Fuck 'em! I happen to like the look of my boy piss-soaked."

Then without warning, Mack grabbed the back of Gregory's' head and shoved his tongue down the boy's throat.

"You did well, boy…" Mack said.

Gregory smiled. Within his head he wondered what he had gotten into with this man. But for now, It didn't matter. He wasn't about to stop now. His cock shivered at the prospect of the bonfire.

They climbed onto the bike and flew back onto the highway, never noticing the trucker and his partner walking out to a large 18 wheel truck. The tattooed trucker got on his cb radio and said calmly.

"Master Wolf come back…"

"Master Wolf here..."

"The boy is coming to the fire, Sir."

"Excellent news, see you and your cub tonight, Bear. Master Wolf out."

A Boner Book

1707, VIRGINIA

It was the way that the fields of wheat seemed to bend in the wind that had always given Mack a joy of living in Kansas. Of course, there were other reasons that kept him in the prairie state. Since the late 1700s he had been in service to Wolf, and partnered with Shields for many of those years. It was not something anyone really had planned. But love is rarely something that one decides in advance.

A month after he arrived in Virginia those many years ago, MacElroy, Shields, and several other folk headed out to the Mississippi River. It would be several weeks from Richmond and the fertile soils of the tobacco farms, before they reached the Mississippi River. Long days of travel through rough terrain were followed by nights of deep sleep. Mack marveled at the greenery that greeted them along the way. But what he didn't really adapt to was the humidity.

"Yer in the wet country here, boy," Shields said with a smile.

"Is it always like this?" Mack responded.

"Well, the moist air doesn't ever really go away, but you don't want to make this trip in the summer months, it gets really sticky. Two men might not come back apart after mating," Shields replied, winking at the younger Brethren.

Mack found himself slowly becoming attached to the older man. He had known there were some among the Brethren that accepted men interacting with men. In fact, that is what first set him on his journey. Europe had its tolerances, but Mack found himself wanting to explore a new world, with new possibilities. He also found that the idea of exploring that great land with Shields was becoming an increasingly wonderful idea as well. Affection was not something that Mack was accustomed to receiving. The gentle but firm touch of the plantation owner was a source of great joy.

"You know they say that cotton could advance on tobbacer as an export from Virginia. Wait 'til you see Wolf's cotton fields. We sit on a wonderful age of trade between tobbacer and cotton. Don't have to worry 'bout much, really. Everything is going quite nicely. Dade will keep the plantation going during my absence. He's good property, and he's a good man to have around as well. There is one day 'head when slaves won't be property no more, and Dade will be there to lead his brothers into freedom,"

Shields's last comment had been overheard by an older man walking alongside the wagon.

"You ain't one of those nigger lovers, are ya?" the man asked.

Shields stopped his wagon and dropped down the ground from his seat.

"I advise you, mister, to watch your tongue. While they might not be on my plantation any longer, but I currently own them in contract, they are good people and I don't take kindly to unfavorable talk. If you do, you can find yer own way to the river, or if you keep yer yakkin' like this, you'll arrive at Fort Adams in pieces in need of a doctor's care, you understand me?"

The older man glared at Shields and stomped off down the road.

"People of this age amaze me, talking about their fellow man like they are less than we are when it's perfect obvious to the contrary!" Shields said sternly.

Mack sat in the wagon with the reigns in his hands. Shields climbed back up to the seat and laughed.

"We aren't gonna get closer to Memphis this way, MacElroy. Get 'em moving again," Shields laughed.

With a shake of the reigns, the two horses began pulling their cart once again.

"Don't worry boy, that man's got enough chips on his shoulder to bury himself with. Life is too short to worry 'bout other people's problems, all you need to worry bout is getting this small shipment of tobaccer to Master Wolf on the river," Shields said as he patted MacElroy on the shoulder.

"But, in a way, I am a slave of Master Wolf, I am indebted to him for the travels, so that makes me like Dade, yes?" Mack questioned

"Ah, but that's different my young friend, Master Wolf doesn't own you outright. The slaves you'll encounter are owned people. Imprisoned from their worlds in the southern continent, and brought here to work for white peoples. It's only going to lead to bad things. While I have slaves on my plantation, Dade takes care of them, and they know I ain't gonna hurt them. They are an important part of my trade; not all "Masters" are that forgiving. And as far as you being in owing to Master Wolf, well, there are a hell of a lot worse places to be, or situations for someone to be in. Wolf is good people. As you'll see. And as for bein' his slave, you made that by choice. In time you'll want to kneel and give yourself to him. You will do it cause your heart tells your too. Dade and his people aren't given choice, some people treat them like cattle. You ain't beef, nor are they..." Shields replied.

"Why is this river we are heading to held in such high regard?" Mack asked.

"Ah, that is the mighty Mississippi!"

"Mighty, huh?"

"You ain't seen a river like it in England, or the continent for that matter. Words don't describe it…"

"Words don't describe it…" came the voice.

Mack returned to the present standing before Wolf's canyon. Looking down on the canyon, the memories of the past now replaced with the human pup settled between his legs... Down in the clearing one could see cars, trucks and bikes arriving.

"This is the bonfire site." Mack said softly into Gregory's ear.

"I'm nervous. You only just met me. I feel like an outsider."

"Don't worry pup, you will fit in just fine."

Mack pulled Gregory's head back and planted a deep kiss, the type of kiss that bonded two men together. Mack was beginning to feel comfortable with the boy. There was part of him that wanted to strip the boy naked right there in the viewpoint and fuck him senseless. But there was time for that type of interaction later. If everything went right, they would have much more time than the boy would think possible. The biker just leaned into the human and took in his scent. A gentle mixture of soap from the shower in the morning, the sweat of the day on his skin, and the reminder of the feeding of piss earlier in the day filled Mack's nostrils.

The scent would be something that could keep him happy for many years to come. He squeezed tighter and hoped that in the coming days, the human might feel the same.

Gregory felt the passion in the kiss and couldn't help be overwhelmed by it. The adventure with this biker was quietly rotating between incredibly intense and wonderfully gentle. He half expected to wake up from this dream any moment. His car would still be broken down, and the future would be bleak. For now however he would not complain about the state of things. There was this voice in the back of his head that asked about the logistics of the feelings that were brewing. He was on his way to Dallas, and now he was quickly bonding with a biker in the middle of nowhere in Kansas.

"So this is like a bike run?" Gregory asked.

The biker smiled. The biker smiled, but Gregory sensed that there was some much deeper secret lying deep beneath that enigmatic smile.

"It is a tad more than that, but you will need to find out for yourself."

CHAPTER FOUR

Master Wolf lay in his bed, watching the ceiling fan cut through the fog of smoke that lay in the room. The two slaves lying within reach were softly sleeping in the morning light. He puffed on his pipe deeply and released his smoke down upon the two men in bed with him. The two men shifted in their sleep, and one seemed to almost show arousal from the smoke surrounding him. Wolf smiled.

It was the silent moments in his life that Wolf really treasured. Sure, there was time for loud and boisterous, like the evening ahead at the bonfire. But, silence allowed Wolf to reflect.

Many memories of being alive for close to 975 years filled his mind. From the burning of birth on another continent, well past watching his parents die during the Black Plague, and the anger at the disease leaving him different that most. Brethren survived the plague in the same determination that mankind did. After the plague, when the world entered its first "Renaissance", was when others began to notice a change in Wolf. He had suddenly become a forecaster. He could see glimpses into the future which, even for one of the Brethren, were considered disturbing. With one touch of another person, he would be able to firmly determine the year of their passing, and whether there would be a human partner with them during their passing into aging. It was a trait his Mother had possessed but kept secret. Now the fevers of the plague had awakened the future sight within him.

But man's joy of life didn't last long. Like always, another plaque would befall man. Filled with jealousy man nor Brethren can stay in a renaissance forever. They eventually succumb to an equally deadly as the plaque.

War in Europe. It was there that man called The Crusades that eventually led Wolf to Ireland. It was there that he found others in the Brethren community that seemed to have grown in power since the plague. It was there he learned of his ability to teleport. It was there that he first met MacElroy's father.

Thomas Tanner had taken in Wolf as a young apprentice. Thomas and his wife soon discovered that Wolf was different from others. They were at dinner and Thomas's wife laid her hand on Wolf's in greeting. Wolf stiffened. Flashes of images filled his mind. He saw many things. He shuddered and ran to his small quarters.

Soon after, Thomas Tanner came to his bedside, and asked him what was wrong.

"I can't explain, Thomas, I see things..."

Thomas rubbed his beard.

"I see..."

Wolf turned away from him. Thomas went to touch him on the shoulder and recoiled.

"You are a future-seein' one, aren't you?"

Wolf didn't answer.

Thomas laughed.

"You don't really think that I didn't a sense a difference in yeh? Did you now?"

Wolf turned to his elder in surprise.

"If you saw the future, lad, I want to know what you saw."

Thomas's wife appeared in the doorway. For Thomas, Susan had been the light of the world to him. There never another in his heart.

"Seeing into one's future isn't right," she murmured.

Thomas turned to her.

"Susan my dearest, If you don't want to hear your future, then turn away, woman. I want to hear what the forecaster has to say."

Wolf turned to the woman.

"I'm sorry I didn't mention it before, Ma'am."

The woman's stern look melted to a gentle smile. She came and sat next to her husband.

"Tell us of the future you saw..."

Wolf took a deep breath.

"You'll have three sons."

The woman smiled.

"The first born will not be an average member of the clan. He will be…different."

"Different, how?" the wife asked.

"He will become the type of Brethren that never find a woman's love and sire children."

Thomas stared at Wolf with cautious eyes.

"Go on…"

"It will be three hundred years before the birth of your third child, and both your other children will live to find a new world, a world full of new futures beyond counting…"

Thomas's eyes grew wide with interest.

"There are other worlds out there?"

"I would not have thought it possible either 'til she touched my hand. A land with Brethren of a completely different clan than our own. Brethren who believe in a different set of Gods. And have a communal nature about them, They have many original new names about them. Ah…rap…aho, Nav…aho…different languages they have."

Wolf closed his eyes. He seemed to wince, but finally went on. "Your family line has a great future in the second son."

The woman smiled gently. "It is told there is always the sad ending to your futures…that you literally see death," she prompted calmly.

"I ne'er like telling folk of their deaths…"

The woman reached calmly forward and reached out to his hand.

"Then show me..."

Wolf pulled his hand away from her. The woman could visibly sense his resistance.

"I meant no harm..." Susan said softly.

"Touching is the connection, I just need to be more prepared when entering another's thoughts and experiences M'am," Wolf said.

He slowly reached to her hand. He could feel her heartbeat faster as his hand reached for her skin. He turned to her eyes, seeing the apprehension and fear.

"Then we begin..." Wolf whispered.

Their hands came together. The Tanner home vanished around them, and the Susan and Wolf were upon a hill in a unknown land. Upon the hill stood three figures. One was obviously Thomas Tanner, and the other two were unknown to either of the travelers. When Thomas turned towards them, his hair was grey. Signs of age were all over his face but gentle nature of her husband remained.

"Can they see us?" the woman asked.

"No, the future cannot see the past."

He stood on the ocean cliff, before a small burial. The youngest of the three people knelt at the grave and spoke softly. She had the same blonde hair as Susan.

"Susan Tanner, this day of our lord, 13th of October 1675. may the fires of this land take her soul and cleanse..." The young lady spoke as she laid a flower upon the grave.

1675. Two hundred years from where they has began.

"Two hundred years..." Susan gasped. "Two hundred more years. look how young Molly has grown!"

Thomas put his hand on the young Brethren's shoulder and sighed.

"Iceland has been good to us, and she was good to Iceland."

"She still wishes she could have found where the forecaster went."

"Maybe we'll never know where Wolf landed when he vanished that day..."

"But he was a forecaster?" the second younger male Brethren asked.

"Oh yes—and who knows: perhaps one day you'll meet our forecaster!"

"It seems so far off, Father..."

"I understand MacElroy, but one day we'll be where he took himself. "

"You seem so sure of the future, Father."

"Everything the forecaster predicted has come true in many ways,"

The scene changed to a hectic house scene. Their home had never had so many people in it. Midwife's running back and forth with water.

"She is giving birth," rose a voice.

Susan then turned around to see herself giving birth. The burst of energy filling the house as her son was born. The sign of a Brethren being born washing over everyone within its walls. The Father of the Tanner Clan kneeling proudly at her side.

"We shall name him MacElroy, and he'll be strong!"

The numerous people in the home shouted in celebration.

The house reformed around the forecaster and the woman. Susan Tanner smiled and turned to her husband.

"You'll be very handsome with grey in your hair," she said.

"Don't be daft in front of our guest," Thomas said sharply to his wife.

"So I am to have three healthy children. And find myself in a new land. It was thermal Thomas, steam coming from all around us. Green cliffs like we have never seen in the isles."

Thomas smiled at his wife.

"It is only proper that you let me see my future as well, forecaster…"

Wolf seemed resistant.

"My only fear is that it will change my training and you'll interact with me differently."

"No fears young one. There are others here among us who will never sire children. They are good people, and will be able to assist both my young one and yourself."

Susan laughed.

"One does notice you are attentive to my husband, and not as much to me, as most men of your age are. We are not naïve, young one."

Thomas reached out his hand, and Wolf met it halfway. Once again the home vanished around them, and Thomas's wife with it.

They stood in a valley. Mountains taller than any they had seen. Cold crisp air filled their lungs as they saw the landscape. In the distance, bubbling streams and green lush fields. Just like the vision of the woman's vision, the world around them seemed covered in cold fog, and the warm descent of steam all at once.

Wolf then noticed the single Brethren standing before them. The man standing on the cliff was Thomas. He was much older now. The grey had become white. As he stood at the Susan's gravesite, he bent over, showing signs of great age.

Thomas from the present gasped at the sight.

"I have done everything you ever asked of me, forecaster. It has been 40 years since my loving wife left us. MacElroy was sent on the ship as you instructed. He has been gone near 12 years now, after we got your post from the ships returning from the new world. You must have a good grasp on instruction now, the young lad that brought your message was quite well behaved. He has been trained well.

He is working in the fields with Hamilton and Seth. My second and third born will be here for many seasons to come. They are on the safe side of the isle.

So I send you my firstborn. He is exactly as you forecast, and will find comfort once in your company, just as we did. You will comfort him in his loss. He still mourns his mother. He will need your guidance, and your companionship. Times have changed, and even among Brethren, MacElroy needs to be with his own kind. It is good of you to keep him away from the possibility of persecution, to wait for the day where worry will be for naught. He is on his way to Master Shields in Virginia.

And I don't know if you hear these words or not," the Thomas in his vision turned to look at them directly. For a moment it seemed he the two men were there.

"I have dreaded this day, but also know: one does not escape the future. It will only haunt you 'til it comes true. I know you are there..."

The old man laughed.

"You were well to us Master Wolf...and to you Mr Tanner...it is strange talking to me...take care of Susan while you have here. There is great joy ahead here in Ireland."

With that final statement the world around them burst into flame and gas. The older vision of Thomas burst into millions of little pieces as the two men found themselves surrounded by a wall of ash and fire. Wolf and Thomas found themselves in the center of a volcanic eruption.

The cabin suddenly appeared around them as Wolf released Thomas's hand.

"There are reasons I don't like doing that…" Wolf gasped still having the taste of ash in his mouth.

Thomas was white as a sheet.

"Well that is not a pleasant experience," Thomas said calmly, then turned to his wife.

"I will live 40 years after you, and ensure our family is set on their paths."

"Your hand is warm to the touch my husband, what did you see?" the woman said.

"Let us just say, I will die near where you were buried. And I will die willingly and painlessly."

Thomas never talked of the vision again. Neither did Wolf.

PRESENT

Wolf winced as the morning light broke through the shades of the window to his face.

The ever-present leather gloves were placed skin tight over his hands. He had learned gloves could allow him to touch again. He could touch without learning all about the person he interacted with. Though the years, technology made gloves quite comfortable. A glove maker in San Francisco had made then specifically for him. The small plain red "W" on the cuff of each glove made them his favorite pair to wear. There would be a time when he would remove the gloves, but this was not yet the time.

There would come a time quite soon where the gloves would be removed and he would peer into the future again. He was to ensure that this human he had seen in visions regarding Mack was the one to bring his young protégé peace.

For now, the past lay behind him, where it belonged. The time for remembering was over. The young human was coming soon. Sadly, that meant no feeding for the slaves who were now awakening around him. They would not be pleased. Good thing that slaves didn't always get what they wanted. It was the nature of things.

But the past sometimes seemed unfair. Sometimes, even for Masters, life wasn't always perfect.

KAINTUCKS. EARLY 1800S

Master Wolf remembered when Brethren and Indians for the most part lived in peace. Most Brethren kept their distance and enjoyed the silence that the river provided. But all that changed when Europeans eventually arrived in the new world and claimed it for themselves. Those that made it through the Appalachians to Ohio eventually got that itch that man always gets to move on, and established the Natchez Trace. Leading from Ohio to the Mississippi River through what would later be known as Tennessee, through the wilderness to the ports of Natchez and New Orleans on the big river, it was the "highway" of its age. The people who traveled those parts had a name. Those travelers were called Kaintucks. With the people from the North eventually came people from the Southern states as well. Virginia and Georgia brought another brand of people. They would eventually change a lot of people's lives. But when Master Shields and the new young Brethren named MacElroy arrived in new city of Memphis, war would soon drive their lives north. The argument over slavery made many people lose their minds with hatred and bigotry. Those very emotions would cost someone very close to them all his life. The battle over of Memphis made it certain that Wolf's clan of Brethren needed to move north and find a quieter area of the world. Master Wolf thought that Kansas City and St Louis would be far enough way from the bloodshed and horrors of a war that tore the new country apart for so long. He regretted to this day that he would be wrong. Hatred had no boundaries.

1863, LAWRENCE, KANSAS

Time had a way of slipping through one's fingers. Growing tensions drove Wolf to relocate to a more northern climate. The south was preparing to boil over into conflict, and Wolf wanted to be far away from it. In the valleys of wheat fields and thunderstorms the clan found their home. Within a day's reach of the Missouri River, Wolf found the haven of Lawrence. The railroad had reached Kansas City and for Wolf it was like being back in the frontier. This would be the place that American Clan of Brethren would call home for many years. From their humble ranch they would greet visitors, provide shelter, and Master Wolf would first find himself being the host. Wolf's Outpost was opened in 1861. Wolf was home. For him there would be no more wandering. The plains that surrounded Kansas City were his home. When the states were created around them, the subject of slavery returned to their lives. Master Shields was to have none of it.

"To make a people decide on whether we are a slavery state or an abolitionist state is just something that just ain't right, Wolf, and you know it." Shields had said.

"Now you keep those thoughts to yourself youngun, it aint been more than 2 years since the end of the blazing time, and we don't need to go starting it up again." Wolf answered.

Shields stormed off to the barn. Wolf stood on the porch of the home he had built with the man now walking away from him, with a heavy heart. It had been almost 80 years that young MacElroy and Shields had come to be with Wolf. While homosexuality was something that wasn't talked about, the three men had a good life. The inclusion of women in the household, even women who had men as partners created a small community that created family with no boundaries. MacElroy found the new world enthralling. Much to Wolf's enjoyment most people round their shop started calling him Mack. Mack seemed to fit the young handsome man much more than his formal name.

A majority of the slaves had come from Shields plantation in the eastern states when Shields sold it. They stayed on to work the wheat, and start a savings. Shields had insisted upon it. Wolf had always tried to keep an even keel when it dealt with the issue of "owning" another. There was a difference between owning a man because he willfully gave himself to you. Wolf had bonded with Mack to the point that the young man would give his life to protect Wolf. Mack was his slave in all accountabilities, but it creates a relationship just as deep as any other type of marriage. "Slavery" as southerners defined it was owning someone just because they were brought on a ship and sold. Owning someone against his will was something Wolf could never consider. He just chose to be less vocal about it than Shields. But as the Civil War exploded, even the edge of the new society wasn't immune. The year after their relocation the war burst through the waters of Memphis as Union forces defeated the Confederate army. The Battle of Memphis would bring the war upstream and be an event that the clan would never forget.

The slavery issue never seemed to go away. Wolf had found solace in the knowledge that their local senator was an abolitionist. But as history has repeatedly shown, hate and desperation always seem to lead to pain and suffering by the innocent. Blood would be shed, and not just by humans.

It was the screaming voice of Shields in the darkness of the hot summer night. Shields came running into the main house screaming, "My God they are killing people, burning buildings! We have to stop them!" Wolf ran to the door to see smoke in every direction; it looked as if all of Lawrence had caught on fire at once. Screams filled the glowing amber sky. The city that had called home seemed to all on fire at once. Everywhere they looked flames were climbing skyward licking the darkness of night.

For Wolf, the screams were familiar. Screams he had forgotten about but knew were coming nonetheless. Wolf stood on the porch, terrified. His visions were becoming reality, but for the first time, he was actually inside one of his visions. The flames. The screaming. Wolf knew what was coming, but still he ran for his guns and to wake Mack to assist in protecting their outpost.

Wolf and Mack made it halfway across the clearing between the house and the outpost when the fire erupted in the hay. A man on a horse rode away with several other torches in his hand. Guns were being fired in the air. Wolf kept running into the horrific scene unable to find direction. So much of their lives was quickly burning away. They ran through the gate leading from the homestead toward the outpost. Wolf had seen in his vision became reality as the fields of hay around the outpost burst into raging flames. He watched Shields in front of the store, getting all the staff safely out of the building.

As he saw Shields hurry three black women into the clearing, Wolf turned to Mack and ordered his slave into action.

"Get those women to safety, they are not safe here."

Mack stood almost hypnotized by the flames.

"Mack! Now!"

Mack answered with a simple "Yes SIR" and ran for the women as Wolf ran to the front of the store. In front of the store, there were two other men on horseback, chasing the women across the square.

"Stand down, men!" Wolf commanded.

The two men turned to Wolf, figuring that taking on the owner of the land was an even better target, when a single gunshot filled the air.

"I think you better do what the man says." Shields said. He stood on the front porch of the outpost with his long shotgun.

"Now, I have one more bullet. I dont think you two want to figure out who I shoot dead and who I let live 'til I can get more," Shields added.

Wolf felt the heat of the fire growing. The two men flew out of the square on their horses and Shields sighed in relief. Wolf then saw the fire's goal.

"Get the kegs out!" Wolf cried out. Forever afterward, he would never know whether Shields had heard him or not.

Shields relief soon turned to fear as he also saw the path of the fire: the ten kegs full of gunpowder, directly to his left. He turned to Wolf with a pleading eye as the first explosion ripped through the store. Wolf could do nothing but watch as the inferno ripped through the store, then tore through his partner of so many years.

For the first time, Wolf himself was living through one of his visions coming true. Time seemed to slow down. The flames licked around Sheat's body. There was a single tear in the man's eye as the flames engulfed him and the explosion took his body apart. The handsome man simply vanished in the exploding barrels of gunpowder. There was no pain. Shields simply wasn't there any more. Mack came running up to Wolf, and the Master grabbed his slave and held him.

"But Shields is in there!"

Wolf held tightly onto his partner, and cried into the night sky. "Not any more, he isn't…"

Mack's knees buckled under him at these words, and he collapsed to the ground, holding his master's leg, and crying with him in the night. With the last explosion of the gunpowder, the outpost was demolished. Master Shields was gone to the wind of the plains. Wolf could still hear the cries of pain from Mack as they watched the pieces from the outpost fall from the sky. The Lawrence Massacre claimed one of the clan. The survivors would never be the same.

CHAPTER FIVE
PRESENT

Master Wolf stood on the clearing above the bonfire where he found Mack and the human slave boy sleeping soundly under the stars. Memories flowed around him. History is harder to forget when you experience more of it than many have. Master Wolf was wise enough to know that the future of his clan lay in the pair under the blanket, huddled in the darkness gaining warmth from each other. The new human clinging to Mack's arm like a teddy bear. Mack was close to 800 years old now, and Wolf was ready to pass on his legacy as clan leader. No one lived forever, not even the original generation of Brethren. But before Wolf left this world and passed on to the next, a new pair of Brethren must mate. They would gain the burden of living for 3000 years. As with every gift, there was a price; nothing came free. Soon Mack would need to wear gloves to prevent him from seeing everyone's past and future, whether he wanted to or not, and the slave boy would have to make a choice. Everyone makes choices, and soon both the handsome brethren whom Wolf had watched mature and his human companion would mature quickly as the days grew long. They would be at the edge of a new generation of Brethren.

Kansas would still be their home. Wolf knew that. Now he would need to touch the human to make sure that the whispers of the dead were right. He needed to know that this was the slave they had been waiting for. Wolf quietly walked up to the sleeping couple and removed his leather glove. He placed his hand on the human's skin and the valley seemed to fall away from view. It was time to see more of this slave's life. The caress of pain and the delicious taste of love. It is the kind of pain that one just doesn't talk about. There are sensual pains about which one can write pages upon pages, but pain of the heart is a completely different story---the human's story. Some stories of pain are diluted with moments of humor or irony that allow the pain in the main story arc to be less bitter. But, for Gregory Carter, there was no happy ending to the story thus far. All he heard, and all he sensed was pain.

Wolf reached into the memories of the human gently as to not disturb his rest.

Wolf that knew that the human had pain inside as well. Then Gregory's emotions poured over him...the loss of a partner was still dwelling.

The Master looked down on his slave and the new boy they had found. There would be pain and grief enough for both of them. But together, they had hope of sacrifice for each other, and bonding unlike neither of them had ever experienced. It would be even stronger than the 500-year bond between Mack and Master Wolf. There was only one thing standing in their way: the human learning the truth. Both human and non-human would need to come to grips with the past, if they were to embrace the future. Master Wolf released another large plume of smoke and let the wind carry it away.

But that was for another day coming soon. Now the boy dreamed softly in his new dominant's arms. Wolf walked back into the canyon below in search of an eager throat. The smoke of the late night had aroused him. It was time to feed another and let the two handsome men sleep.

CHAPTER SIX
PRESENT, DAY THREE

Gregory woke once again in the arms of the Mack who had filled the last two days with adventure and a heightened sexual awareness. It was a little disconcerting that Gregory found himself doing many things he had never done. It was like the biker made him lower his inhibitions. He enjoyed the dawn of the new day and also found himself enjoying feeling the gradual wakening of this man who held him in his embrace. The hard cock that brushed against his ass cheeks indicated that the softly rumbling man who had held him in the coolness of night was also awake. Powerful arms tightened around Gregory's body, then slowly turned him around to face the biker who had brought him out to this valley. There was genuine attraction in the large man's eyes. Gregory couldn't argue with the emotion either. It was very strange but the two men had bonded very strongly over the last two days. The strong hand that grabbed the back of his head showed the goal of his awakening partner.

A masculine push against the back of his head led him down under the blanket. His tongue explored the trail of fur on the muscular chest, but it was the hardened cock that was his goal. Gregory worked his tongue over the biker's chest and stomach until the hard inches of cock greeted his mouth.

It seemed much harder to engulf the large pierced head of the biker's cock two days ago when he first tasted the man's flesh. The smooth cool metal of the Prince Albert ring that capped the biker's cock slipped effortlessly down into his throat. Within minutes the piercing was buried deep in his throat, and the man-scented balls brushed against his beard. The hand that had guided him to the biker's cock had not been removed. If anything the calloused hand was even more intent on keeping him to task. As the boy worshipped the biker's cock there would be moments of gagging around the thick piece of meat. This made the biker only push him farther down the cock. There would also be an audible sigh of pleasure as the boy's throat opened to the morning arousal of the biker who was still fully in charge of him. The boy could feel the biker's balls begin to tense up. The biker let up on the firm grip but not enough to allow the boy to take the cock out of his mouth. This was cock worship pure and simple and Gregory couldnt get enough.

"That's a good boy, take care of Daddy's morning cock. You'll get it every morning from now on," the deep masculine voice of the biker said softly into the morning light.

Gregory continued to worship the biker's cock. Feeling the slight release of the grip each time that release was building. All the boy wanted was his Daddy's cock in his throat. They rode the wave of mansex that flowed over them both. It was a natural thing for the boy to have his Daddy's cock buried in his throat. The biker lay back under the morning sun and just enjoyed the warmth the boy was providing.

The biker reached with his other hand to the boy's ass, and Gregory's furry pucker shuddered at his touch. One finger, then two, slowly made their way into the boy's hole.

"Tonight that hole is going to become mine. I will pound you like no other man ever has, and from that point on you will know me as MASTER."

The grip on the boy's head become firm and unrelenting. Mack could hear Gregory gagging around his cock, and it only made him want to bury it further down the human's throat; to fill it like no one ever had before.

"Now you drink your Master's seed...all of it...drink from the only tap you will ever need," the biker commanded.

Gregory felt his throat shudder around the biker's cock, this cock he couldn't get enough of. He gagged and slurped around the piercing, feeling the biker's grip of the biker intensify, desperately wanting the biker's release to be poured down his throat. He opened his throat up and took the cock all the way to its base. The finger-fuck invasion of his ass only made him want to suck harder and please the biker even more.

"That's it, boy. Two holes will be mine. That furry ass will get ridden hard. My seed will pour deep into your bowels, and you'll be mine. You want it, don't you?"

The boy could only suck and slurp in response.

"Yeah, that's what I thought, boy. Now, take that cock over the edge and empty my balls. Knowing the next time they release, they release into your ass."

The boy felt the massive furry balls tense up one last time. The spasm of that sexual edge finally being crossed opened up his holes, and with the PA diving deeper into his throat, he could feel the globs of cum pouring down his gullet. The worship he provided prevented him from noticing the third finger invading his ass. The roar as the biker fed the boy his seed could be heard all over the valley, and brought several cheers of congratulation from the other encampments around the valley. The vibration of the biker's cock sent shock waves through the boy's body as it slowly withdrew from the boy's throat and landed the PA on his tongue. As more seed dribbled from the cock head onto his tongue the boy was content.

"Yer not done yet boy," the biker said firmly.

The hand that was firmly invading his ass pressed forward. With all the biker's strength he pushed and slid the boy back up his own body.

"Get that cock up here, boy. You need draining."

The boy had actually forgotten about his own cock in the need to serve the biker. The half fist in his ass made it hard not to comply with the biker's wishes. His cock was brought up to the biker's chest, with the hand still firmly in his ass.

"Empty your balls onto my beard, boy."

Gregory obeyed. He took a hold of his cock that already firm and dripping precum. The biker lurched upward, taking one of the boy's nipples into his mouth, then bit down and started to chew on the boy's chest.

"That's it boy: your holes, your nipples, all of you is mine now," the biker said roughly.

It was exhilarating to the boy that the biker had discovered that working his nipples would lead to thick strings of cum sprayed across the older man's beard. There were not many men who actually knew how to work a man's nipples the way the boy liked them worked. It seemed as though this biker was a professional tit worker.

"It wont be long, SIR!" the boy gasped.

"Give me what is already mine, boy," the biker commanded.

The hand in the boy's ass, coupled with the teeth working his chest took the boy beyond any ability to hold back. Thick streams of cum burst out across the biker's chest and beard. With each thrust of the biker's fist in his ass, more of Gregory's seed poured out onto the biker's beard. The hand slowly retreated from the boy's hole and the muscular arms settled the boy beside his Daddy. The man who would soon become his Master. Gregory might have had doubts about the last 48 hours, but it was clear. This biker was unlike any other man he had ever been around.

"Good boy," the biker said softly.

Gregory looked up at Mack to see the thick strands of seed glistening in the morning sun.

"Good boy, indeed."

Gregory fell back to sleep upon his new partner's chest . There would be no more nightmares now. The biker watched the human fall back to sleep in his arms and smiled.

The voices on the wind had been right. This boy was the one meant to take his cock. This human would become his partner. Just the thought of it left the biker with a heavy string of precum from his cock. There was only one obstacle left: Master Wolf would have to meet the human without any shield of deception.

The biker turned to the rest of the valley and saw the rest of the Brethren waking and stirring. There would be plenty of time to mingle and catch up with old friends—some older than others.

Wolf stood on the porch of his cabin and looked back into the living room. Four male slaves in a pile of half-sleep and sexual need was something he never really got over seeing in the morning. Male sexual energy was always a welcome morning greeting. Wolf looked out over the valley. There were several encampments filling the small green valley with visions of the bond of his extended family.

These beings, this race known only as The Brethren: boys and their Owners, Mistresses and their servants, men and women, some of them well over 600 years old, right here in the confines of this valley., but Wolf knew of only five or six with any legitimate claim to being any older: MacElroy, now known as "Mack" in this new age; the trucker Brace; Theodore, the club owner in Vegas; and the mountain man, Alexander. And Patricia, of course—who could forget Patricia, the eldest female in attendance?

As if Wolf had called her name aloud, Patricia's camping trailer opened up and her servant stepped out into the morning light. Wolf stood in the gentle mist of morning as Patricia, the 800 year-old woman herself, stepped out of her trailer, her servant gently letting down the steps so the gentlewoman could step from the trailer to the ground. Patricia turned and said something softly to her servant, then slowly and carefully walked towards Wolf as the servant stepped back into the trailer. She skirted the edges of the other emcampments as she walked up to Wolf and began to speak.

"Good morning, Master Wolf. I wanted to thank you again for your hospitality during our voyage West." the woman said gracefully.

"It is the least I can do for my flesh and blood. You know you are always welcome here," Wolf responded.

"There were times on my journey when I tried to understand how you have lived so many more years than I could ever imagine," the old woman said, shaking her head in wonder. "But know, as I enter my twilight, that your guidance of the North American Brethren has been proper and bold. Even through thin times."

Wolf smiled.

"Again, you are too kind, Mistress Patricia. Your father was one of my best friends for many years. Your family is always welcome among our clan. Although there are times that I feel your servant doesn't quite know what to do with all the homosexuals lusting after him."

Patricia laughed.

"Well, my being one of the only heterosexual Mistresses within two hundred miles of him does add a new touch of devotion to his service..." the woman laughed.

Wolf laughed with her.

"You have entered your 800's with grace and beauty, Patricia," Wolf said softly.

"There were times I never thought I would reach these years."

"The plague was quite a way to spend one's Brethren youth, wasn't it?" Wolf asked.

"You, of all people, know of this. We are rare," Patricia responded.

"But here we are in a world where mankind is once again growing in leaps and bounds. Sexuality is becoming less of a question as the years go on. Just look at San Francisco and New York."

"That is actually where I am heading: San Francisco. My nephew has decided to make the city his home, and I owe him a visit."

"And how is Maximilian?" Wolf said with a smile.

"Lonely...but you know, that is as much his fault as anyone else's. But he loses himself in the city that allows one to do so."

"Please give him my best. "

Patricia's servant had once again emerged from the trailer, this time with a silver coffee pot and several cups. He stepped up to the two elder Brethren and knelt.

"Coffee is ready, Madam." the servant announced.

"Excellent. You made good time of it. Wolf, would you like a cup?"

Wolf never said no to a good cup of coffee.

"I would be most grateful."

The servant placed two of the coffee cups on the porch and filled them both with dark rich coffee, handing one to Patricia and the second to Wolf.

"I see you still prefer your coffee dark and bitter," Wolf said with a smile.

"Is there any other way to have coffee first thing in the morning?" Patricia answered.

Suddenly, there was a loud and exhilarating howl from the bluff above them. Wolf knew that howl better than most. "MacElroy is awake," he commented to Patricia, raising one eyebrow.

"I hear he has found a good boy," Patricia said enthusiastically.

"That he has. They are coming to me in the heat of the afternoon today. We will sweat and I will show the slaveboy his future. MacElroy has not had non-gloved interaction with me for a longtime now. He is ready."

Patricia shuddered.

"I find it a very unsettling experience even when sexual intercourse isn't involved. It must be a very intense connection."

Wolf smiled into the morning light.

"Not very different, really," Wolf said with a smile.

"You were never very good at lying to me, Wolf."

Wolf laughed as Patricia's servant arrived and stood in front of them.

"Attend to breakfast then, Charles. We'll depart at 11 a.m." Patricia made it clear that this was more than merely a suggestion. Her servant bowed politely and returned to the trailer silently.

"He is very good at presentation," Wolf said as he drank his coffee.

"He knows he result if he isn't. But yes, Charles pleases me immensely."

The Master and Mistress continued to talk as the sun rose and the community of Brethren slowly woke up around them. Patricia had to admit that Wolf had a broad and unique clan. The working class of the Midwest, with everything from wheat farmers to truck drivers talking among themselves with CB radios, and even the occasional city folk. So many clans in the cities tended to be modern and lacked that "traveled" look of Wolf's clan. There was just something to said about the unshaven non-conformist of the men around Wolf. It showed sharp contrast to her upbringing in Europe.

Wolf stood on his doorstep and saw the two men on the hill above rise from their slumber. The three of them would bond, and sooner rather than later; Wolf was sure of this. His cock rose under his jeans just thinking of being close to Mack again. Mack had always had that effect on him. It wasn't just the agreement he had made with the man's parents back in the old country and it only grew stronger when Shields passed away.

From the moment that MacElroy Tanner had arrived, Wolf knew he was different. It wouldn't be until years after Shields's passing, that the two of them, Wolf and MacElroy, would bind a relationship. Wolf was fully aware that Mack had never really let go of Shields, but the young man had chosen to stay with Wolf after the raid on Lawrence. They knew, however, that Lawrence could no longer be their home. Wolf chose to move farther west, but not as far as the higher plains where Denver was becoming a metropolis. They found a new parcel of land on the west prairie of Kansas, along the trade routes that were slowly migrating west. A new general store, a blacksmith's shop, a couple of other storefronts, and the clan quietly became part of Goodland, Kansas.

"So just how old are you, Master Wolf?" MacElroy, the Brethren youth, asked his Master one hot summer day.

Wolf smiled and chuckled softly, chewing the bit of his pipe as he released a fragrant cloud of smoke and prepared his pup for his answer. "Well, it's the damnedest thing for a Brethren elder, I guess, but I reckon my life by human history. I was born in 1054. Nothing special about that year --- 'cept me, of course," and here Wolf grinned broadly at his pup, "but I arrived in the British Isles at the same time as the Norman Conquest: 1066. Didn't make it over to Ireland for some time after that. After the plague..." His voice trailed away in the mists of memory.

"But Master, how do you find yourself...well...not letting the years get to you?"

Mack's question brought Wolf back from his reverie, and he sighed deeply before answering. "I have been a very lucky man, pup. While there are many elders around the world, surviving history is not something I would wish on many people. Those of us with 900 years or more are a royal bunch. You'll be there, and the history behind you when you reach my years will fill your mind with memories as well. You accept your place in the world, and learn to accept death and the passing of those who are not like us."

"May I ask one other thing, Master Wolf?" Mack asked.

Wolf smiled at his young friend. "You are welcome to ask me

anything you wish, young one."

"Why do you wear gloves?"

After the older man's detailed answer about his birth and youth, Mack was surprised when Wolf answered this question with a simple, "I am a seer."

"Yes, Master? A seer…and? Mack prompted.

"Interacting with people after becoming a seer means covering one's hands with leather to prevent unwanted connections from being made, seeing things that are perhaps best left unseen." Wolf suppressed a shudder, but Mack could see that the older man was troubled by memories of scrying sessions that had evidently not been pleasant. Still, Mack could not help himself, and before he knew it he had blurted out yet another question.

"It must be leather, then? Not cloth, or anything else?"

"The power of the vision comes through, and will simply burn away anything but leather. It can be.....intense," Wolf said slowly, examining his own gloved hands.

"I had heard of seers, and Shields had mentioned your abilities in this area. Does everyone become a seer with age?" MacElroy asked.

Wolf seemed to come to himself at his, and became much more matter-of-fact. "Actually no, seers are rare. It was not one of the normal abilities of Brethren before the plague. The fever gave some of us the ability to see, Although I wouldn't' recommend experiencing the plague specifically to become a seer. It is not always the best of things to be able to see into another's future."

"Master?"

Wolf turned to the young man and frowned. "You see futures like Shields's. You see the death. you see the pain, and sometimes you get horrifying visions of where the world is heading, and you don't have a choice in the matter. Seeing isn't a controllable sensation. The future shows you only what you need to know, it isn't a "guidable" vision of everything that is coming for us."

Mack sighed.

"So both you and Shields knew he would die in an explosion?"

"No, we both knew fire would be involved. There are moments that we get to see when we interact with the person and experience it with them. I knew there would be a day when i would be looking at flames around Shields's handsome face. You don't get a "day stamp"; you just know it is coming at some point."

"I would like to see, Master Wolf, Sir."

Wolf abruptly turned on his heel and began walking away from the handsome young man.

"No. In all the years since Shields's passing, I have not removed these gloves, because I don't care to ever again know how others die. It is too difficult."

The young Brethren knelt before the Master.

"I wish to bind to you, Sir. I felt that i needed to bond completely."

Wolf stopped walking, as suddenly as he had begun. He had not expected Mack's line of questioning to lead to bonding, and he turned to face his young companion with a look of intense seriousness on his craggy face.

"If I lead you to the barn and take your holes as mine, you will be mine. Period. There won't be any more trips into the hills to find Indians. You will be mine. My bond with you will be unbreakable."

"I know the results of my request all too well, Sir. Shields spoke of it often."

Without a word, Wolf once again began to walk away from the young man.

"I want to feel your cock inside me, and your bare hands against my skin," MacElroy called out firmly.

Mack's outcry brought Wolf to a dead stop. At last, he turned to face the younger man, then slowly raised one gloved hand and beckoned Mack to come to him. As the Brethren pup drew close, Wolf looked deeply into Mack's eyes and knew his statement to be true. With another deep sigh, Wolf began to speak, slowly and firmly.

"Fetch my cigars... I know over the years since Shields has passed that you have enjoyed being my sexual partner. But if I mount you without the gloves, you aren't a partner any more. You will be my bonded property."

The young Brethren took a deep breath.

"I understand the gift that I give you..."

"It is a gift, isnt it, slave? You will be mine. and my control over you will be quite intense and utterly unforgiving..."

"I want to give myself to you," MacElroy repeated softly.

"Send a message to Frederick Bear in Kansas City. We will need the services of a Brethren guide. If this is to happen, we will need to have someone to bring us back to the present once our bond is complete."

"Yes, SIR!"

The young Brethren ran off to the post office on the rail line. It would take four days for the message to reach Bear, and for Bear and his partner to come to the outpost. Wolf enjoyed seeing the excitement engulf the slaveboy.

"I will claim you, and we will spend hundreds of years together," Wolf whispered into the wind.

MASTER WOLF now stood on the porch of their home from those years ago, and remembered the future that the winds of the prairie had shown them. He had seen Gregory over a hundred years before his car broke down on the freeway. Three Brethren knew that the car would eventually empty its transmission all over the road. Wolf had ensured that the door key to the hotel room had been given to the boy incorrectly. He had a physical shiver when the boy first walked into his cafe two days ago. But it finally had come to pass and now that very slaveboy was heading to the cabin to meet Wolf for a second time.

Master Bear was on his way to the house as well from the other side of the valley. It was always difficult to shield Wolf's arousal from his clan. The growing waves of erotic energy Wolf sent out made most heads turn in his direction, so it would be good to have Bear there to shield others from the fierce erotic pulses. Even now, in fact, Patricia shuddered beside him.

"I see where your morning is heading, Wolf. Perhaps I shall depart a tad sooner."

Wolf turned to her and smiled. "You are welcome to stay."

Holding up a finger, Patricia interrupted him. "Dont misunderstand; I am very happy for you in this day, but the wash of energy that is about to pour over this valley is not the kind I am able to appreciate. I have no complaints or quarrels with homosexual Brethren, but the energy fills me with images that I prefer to leave in your hands. Not to mention what it does to my servant!" she said firmly.

"I understand, Patricia. Safe travels westward."

Patricia stepped off Wolf's porch and started towards the trailer and truck. Her servant stepped out of the trailer anticipating her approach, and was already preparing for departure.

"Good day to you and yours, Wolf," Patricia called over her shoulder, with a wave of farewell.

Wolf bowed silently. Her servant opened the passenger door of the truck attached to the trailer, and Patricia slid into her seat and the servant walked around to the driver's seat.

"Wolf has private business to attend to." Patricia said softly. She turned to her servant and smiled.

"This slave had noticed the increased tension in the air, Mistress," Matthew replied.

The truck and trailer pulled out of the flat space they had kept for the night. Wolf watched as his old friend and her servant left the valley. Bear and his partner came to his side as the trailer pulled over the edge of the hill, and out of sight.

"Mistress Patricia is well?" the tattooed trucker asked.

"She is very well; she heads to San Francisco to look in on Maximilian," Wolf answered.

"Oh, I'm sure he'll just love that!"

"Be mindful of your elders, Master Bear." Although Wolf said it with a laugh Bear became aware that the claw marks of his tattoo had begun to throb, just a little. He took the hint.

Bear's partner came with the large case and knelt beside Bear.

"Master Bear, is your boy trained in the restorative arts?"

"He is. He's actually a nurse in Cheyenne. The cub has served me well these years."

Wolf turned to speak directly to the cub. "It is good of you to keep up the arts young one, they will come in handy this day."

The boy turned his face upwards to the two Masters standing above him.

"It's my honor to serve, Sir."

Bear turned with a smile to his partner. He always got off on the cub's ability to have graceful manners even when the rising sexual energy showed the shape of the day ahead for all of them.

"Go into the main hall, prepare what you need, and be naked by the time your Master and I join you," Master Wolf commanded.

"Yes, Sir!" was the response, and the cub headed into the cabin house.

Bear came up to the porch and looked out on the valley. There were easily 40 men nestled in campsites across the valley. Seeing Mack and Gregory on the hill above, Bear smiled, remembering his interaction with the two men at the freeway rest stop.

"He is a good pup. I think he will match MacElroy very nicely."

"I know he will, Master Bear," Wolf answered with a wry smile.

Bear turned in surprise. "This is something from your bonding with Mac? What are you not telling me?"

"Just be prepared for several intense waves of energy this morning, Bear. Things will be changing, left and right."

Bear smiled. Wolf could see the arousal effecting both them. Bear was never one who could hide arousal.

"Go join your cub, and we will be in shortly."

Wolf watched Mack and Gregory step down from the hill and make their way toward him. He could see Mack introducing the boy to friends as they walked through the various campsites. With a sidelong glance at Mack and his pup, the elder Master held up his hand to signal Bear to wait, then carefully removed his gloves and turned to the trucker.

"There are things you need to know..."

Wolf held one bare hand against the trucker's arm, and it was almost if Bear's tattoos rippled as their flesh came into contact. Bear flinched several times as a wave of pure sexual energy flooded from Wolf's flesh to his. A stream of piss trickled down the trucker's leg and pants as the connection continued.

"Now you understand..." Wolf said he came closer to Bear.

The trucker trembled under Wolf's touch. The two men kissed

and Bear continued to tremble, even more violently. Wolf released his hand from the trucker's arm but continued to kiss the man, as Bear reached around Wolf and pulled him into a large hug.

"So it begins..." Wolf whispered.

"Yes Master Wolf, so it does."

CHAPTER SEVEN

The two men walked into the house to find the cub naked, as instructed. The familiar tools of a scrying session were laid out on a table beside the large bed in the center of the room. Bear tore across the room and kissed his partner deeply. The cub began quickly removing his clothes; he knew when his Master was in need of sexual satisfaction. The urine-soaked pants soon were removed, revealing the truckers fat uncut cock for the cub to take into his throat. Wolf heard the familiar moan of satisfaction as Bear filled his partner's throat with the arousal that only "seeing" could produce.

Wolf saw his three slaves knelt along the wall on the far end of the room, silent, with their forearms flat on the floor,providing full access to their privates for their owner. Wolf stepped over to them and smiled.

"Clothes. But do not come in contact with my hands."

The three slaves leapt from their prone positions and quickly but carefully began to strip their Master of his clothes. Wolf turned to find Bear and his cub fully naked. Bear had found a corner of the bed and held his cub's throat around his cock and laid back in the ecstasy of his cub's ability to worship his cock.

Soon, Wolf was naked as well, his long veiny cock straining for intimacy. Wolf also knew there was only one throat that was going around his cock: that of Mack's new slave. He looked at his servants with great joy. "Enjoy each other during this. The release will be quite wonderful, my boys."

The three slaves didn't need a second command. They started

exploring each other's body on the large mat beside the bed. Wolf reached into the bedside table on the left side of the room, found cigars, and handed one across the bed to Bear.

"Oh god, yes SIR!" Bear said as he took the cigar in his hand.

"That's a good man, Bear, light it up."

Wolf lay back in the center of the bed and leaned up against the bed board when he heard Mack and Gregory approach outside.

Mac came up to the porch of the familiar house and smiled.

"This was our first house when we moved into this part of the world. We have created many memories here," Mack said into Gregory's ear.

"It is a classic," Gregory replied, unsure of how to respond.

"In more ways than you can imagine…"

The biker came up to the porch and then turned to the young pup. "We are going inside to meet Master Wolf. Trust me when I tell you the inside of this house is meant for bonding and sexual interaction. Wolf will be expecting service."

"But we just had sex," the human responded.

"When you are around Wolf, arousal is never an issue. Trust me. And I would imagine Bear will be here again."

Gregory looked at the biker in question. "You mean the trucker and boy from yesterday?"

"Yes boy. You remember he had asked if we were coming to the bonfire this evening?"

"Yes SIR. It will be good to see him again."

"Just be a good boy to Wolf, and all will be fine."

For the first time in quite a while, Gregory was nervous. What exactly were they walking into here? The younger man stepped hesitantly up onto the porch.

Mack smiled at Gregory, with surprising tenderness. "You can be a good boy for me today. I am sure Master Wolf will cherish you as I do."

"Master Wolf?"

"He is the leader of our clan—this group of bikers, truckers, and leathermen you see in front of you. He's...kind of the president of our little club."

"He might not find me attractive, or good enough."

Mack turned to Gregory and smiled.

"There is no reason that Wolf won't like you. But once you are in that house, Wolf is in charge. You do what you are told, and it will go well. Do you understand?"

"Yes Sir."

Mack reached to the boy's hair and ran his hands over the buzzcut scalp.

"Good boy..."

The two men stepped in the front door and Wolf could feel his cock strain at the sight. Mac was covered by a night's worth of sweat, and had the strong scent of the young man standing next to him.

"Welcome to Wolf's Hollow, Gregory." Wolf said softly, reaching to the ashtray and collecting his cigar. He inhaled a deep pull of cigar smoke and held it in to enjoy the tobacco, before releasing a large plume of smoke into the room.

Gregory couldn't shake the feeling that he had seen the MASTER before. The scent that was in the air about him seemed familiar. He couldnt quite place it.

"Well, Let's see more of the boy. strip yourself, you wont be needing those clothes today."

The young human was visibly nervous.

"Don't be nervous with me, boy. No one is going to hurt you. In fact, I think you now understand that hurting you is the least of our intent although I'll admit things can get rough."

Gregory reached for his shirt. It was time for Master Wolf, the Master of his clan, to start making contact with the boy. Master Wolf reached out with his mind and released his arousal into the room. He could see it ripple across everyone as it undulated towards the human boy.

Gregory had found himself almost immediately aroused when he walked into the room. Three furry men nestled together on a lower mat, and seeing the trucker and his partner feeding off each other like time had never passed from the rest stop. He saw Mack stripping as well, and reaching over to help Gregory out of his clothes. That was when the feeling of electricity first came upon him. It seemed to reach into his skin and heighten his sexual energy.

"Wow. that smoke is heavy."

"Do you not like smoke, boy?" Wolf asked cryptically.

"No, on the contrary, Sir!"

Wolf smiled as he released another plume of smoke into the air through his beard. "That was the right answer boy," he said, patting his upper thigh. "Come now, boy. Get out of yer clothes. I have something that needs your atttention."

Gregory saw the very aroused cock between Wolf's legs. He felt Mack's gentle touch removing his pants to his ankles and helping the boy undress.

"Mack can attest. You'll like being between my legs."

Gregory turned to see Bear handing Mack a freshly lighted cigar of his own.

"Give your boy a nice feeding of smoke, Mack," Wolf commanded.

"Yes Sir. Indeed."

The two men embraced with their hardening cocks brushing against each other. Mac kissed Gregory deeply sending fresh cigar smoke into his lungs. They lingered around the smoke as the arousal grew between them.

"That's a good boy. Now come to me," Wolf said.

Gregory turned towards the Master at the head of the bed and crawled onto the bed.

"I like seeing a slave crawl to me, and settle between my legs."

Gregory found himself drawn to the smoke, to the man, and to the dripping cock between the man's legs. He was unable to say no to the offer of being between those legs. He rested his head where the Master had directed. The fat veiny cock sat well within his vision. He moved towards it.

"Ah, first things first!" the Master said, as the cock was pulled away from Gregory's face by a gloved hand.

"You have been brought here to bond with me, and become my

Mack's partner in the life that we choose. You want that, don't you?" the Master asked.

"Yes I do, Sir," Gregory said softly.

Once within reach Gregory finally realized where he had seen this man before. Memories of the cafe flooded through his head.

"Where are you boy?" the MASTER asked.

"I remember you...you were at the cafe, you were the one who seated us and who walked off with Mack that first night." Gregory answered.

He could feel the large cock pulse against his skin.

"A good observant pup..."

Master Wolf released a large plume of smoke into Gregory's face. Mack watched with almost uncontrolled passion as his MASTER's smoke invaded the human boy and pressed him into submission.

"Yes, we have met before. and now you get to do, what you wanted to do the first time you saw me. You want to serve me...dont you slave?" Master Wolf asked.

"Yes SIR," Gregory whispered.

"Then take my cock into your throat, and listen to my words."

Gregory slid down the man's chest and to the now engorged cock. He took the large cock in his throat and swallowed greedily.

"Dont take to sucking quite yet boy..."

The boy's throat stopped worshipping his cock.

"Enjoy the precum...and listen to my words now slaveboy."

Gregory looked up through the smoke at the MASTER.

Wolf laid his hands on the human and the energy that pulsed through the room was immense.

"We are known as Brethen. The men in this room, and out in the valley are of my clan. Mack has explained this to you. There will be many other things to learn about us first, pup. Many things that may be difficult for you to accept, but accept them you must, if you are to become part of this clan. Are you ready?" And with this, Wolf let out another stream of the smoke that seemed almost to obey his will, to go only where he sent it.

"I...think so, Sir," stammered Gregory.

"You must know so, pup, or it will be no good. I will ask you once more, and if you cannot answer me without hesitation and without doubt, I will have no choice but to send you away. Now, are you ready to learn the truth about this group you would join?" Wolf glared at Gregory, and his gaze seemed to bore right through the boy.

Gregory swallowed hard, then spoke firmly and clearly.

"I am ready, Master Wolf, Sir!"

Wolf leaned back once more, this time directing a halo of smoke around the head of the willing boy. "Very well, then. To begin: our name. We are known as the Brethren. While it might seem just a unique name for a motorcycle club, it is much more. We are not your normal fuckers, slave!" Wolf barked. " We are much more. And it is not by accident that you find yourself here. You were brought here for a reason. Not just my pleasure, or Mack's pleasure. You are here to become part of my clan. My family."

"I understand, Sir," the human answered.

"No, you don't!" Wolf snapped. A moment later he softened, and resumed his explanation. "You understand a part, a small part, but there is a much larger part of who we are that you know nothing about. For that part of who we are, lay back and look into the eyes of the man you have bonded with."

Gregory turned to find the biker fully aroused. There was a fiery passion in his eyes that matched the glowing ember at the tip of his cigar.

"We are not 'human' per se. We are hundreds of years old," Mac began.

"My full name is MacElroy Tanner. I was born in the early 1600s in what you would now call Scotland. Wolf came to my home 20 years before I was born. He met and bonded with my parents. He could see my future through that bond, and I was sent to the new world to be with him once I reached my mature age. To human eyes, I have been 45 since 1650. Master Wolf has been 56 since 1110. Bear has been 49 since 1613 and cub has been 28 since 1745. We are all hundreds of years old."

Gregory first didn't really register the magnitude of what Mack had said. He looked from one man to the other, waiting for one of them to crack a smile and laugh at this joke. It was a joke, right? But none of them smiled, and Gregory noticed himself starting to breathe in short, sharp breaths. What if this was really true?

"What Mack tells you is true. Bringing you here today, was to show you, and to invite you into our family of Brethren."

Gregory then noticed the seriousness in their words.

"Hundreds of years old..." Mac said again.

Wolf looked down with loving eyes at the human, then spoke through a smoky sigh.

"It is easier if I show you, rather than trying to explain any further."

Wolf connected with Gregory. The smoke in the room rippled as the truth of what Mac and Wolf presented poured through the connection with the human and the Brethren Master.

Gregory found himself standing on a cliff with Master Wolf. It was a very disturbing sensation, yet somehow Gregory knew he could trust this powerful shaman, this man --- or something more than merely a man --- he knew as "Wolf".

"This is 1625. Ireland." Wolf said softly.

The two men stood naked as they were in the cabin, but the world around them had vanished.

"This is a dream!" Gregory said loudly.

"No, slave, this is the past."

A man then walked into the clearing with them. There was a familiarity to Mack, but this man was not as tall, and had hair down to his shoulders.

"Thomas Tanner. MacElroy's Father..."

The man walked out to the cliff and turned to them both. "I know you have my son's future in your hands." With this, the cliff then vanished, and Thomas Tanner with it.

Suddenly, Gregory and Master Wolf were on the plantation in Virginia watching MacElroy and Shields making love in the tub of hot water.

"Who is this?" Gregory at last whispered.

"MacElroy's first partner, Shields."

"He is very handsome."

Wolf smiled indulgently. "You can feel MacElroy's emotions, can't you?"

"I can...how is this possible?"

"As I told you, we are not ordinary folk. You are seeing MacElroy's past because we bonded in the late 1800's as Master and slave. In that bonding, I gained all of his memories."

Gregory stood speechless. Would this happen if he were to bond to Mack; would Mack gain all of his memories, too? Would Mack be willing to accept them all, even the painful ones?

The scene changed again, to the city of Lawrence, Kansas. Then to a cornfield, where once again Shields and MacElroy were having sexual intercourse. The sexual energy rippled over Master Wolf and Gregory.

"You are my good boy," Shields said to MacElroy.

"I am yours. Forever," MacElroy replied.

Gregory turned to Wolf and began to cry, a single tear trickling down his cheek. "They were in love. Where is Shields now? Why is Mack with me now?"

Wordlessly, Wolf turned and pointed to the horizon. The two men making love in the cornfields vanished, leaving Wolf and Gregory standing alone among the ears of corn. Suddenly, a huge fire erupted. A torch dropped into the field, lighting the corn on fire. In the distance a gigantic explosion. The emotion of arousal was quickly replaced with despair and pain.

"Shields perished in an explosion. Mack took many years to recover from the loss."

Wolf and Gregory found themselves within a huge batch of flames. The man that Gregory knew as Shields stood with a happy grin on his face. The flames seemed to lick the edges of his flesh. He turned and talked directly to Master Wolf.

"So this is how a century ends: gunpowder. We knew it would be a big bang in the end, didn't we?. Take care of my boy. He deserves many years of love Master Wolf. I will miss you both very much." Shields said as the flames slowly overtook him. It was as if time had slowed down for a moment, as the image of Shields gradually began to merge with the flames.

Wolf said softly to Gregory, "Shields knew how he would die, because when he fully bonded with me, his future and his interactions would be revealed to us both. And we had seen this moment together,".

Shield seemed to struggle to speak to Wolf and Gregory. "I will be the voice of the wind for you both. 'Til the love we shared returns to both of your lives," Shields said to the flames, as they quickly spread over his body. With one last tear, Shields was no longer there. There were only flames.

Gregory and Wolf stood at the foot of a tree. Mack leaned against the tree, slowly carving Shield's name into the trunk, as he spoke. "I am glad you will always be around for me to come talk to. This oak will always show me where my Daddy lies. My one true love."

Wolf sighed, speaking as much to himself as to Gregory. "It would take him 10 years to come to me after Shield's death."

"How is all of this possible?" Gregory asked, receiving no reply.

Abruptly, the memories dissipated and Gregory found himself back upon the leg of the cigar master, with Mack looking down at him.

"We are Brethren. Our lives span 900-1100 years. There are those among us that become "seers". Wolf is a seer. He can view the past and preview the future."

"So all that I just saw...is real?"

Wolf turned down to him and smiled. "Oh yes, young one. All real."

Gregory knew inside that what they were telling was the truth. It was almost too much to take in, but the bare hand on his chest showed him the past of the men sitting in the room.

"But we didn't see Bear there. I dont understand."

Upon hearing his name, Bear turned from the corner of the

bed, and smiled. "Oh, I didn't come in 'til later..." Bear reached out to Gregory...and the visions began again.

1867, MACK AND WOLF BOND.

The light in the room seemed to shimmer, and suddenly Gregory found himself standing next to the bed, rather than kneeling on it in front of Wolf, as he had been. He looked down onto the bed to find Mack where Gregory had been just a moment ago, with Wolf holding a firm grip on the biker's head as he pressed his cock deep into Mack's throat. The grey highlights were gone from Wolf's hair.

Bear stood opposite Gregory, on the other side of the bed. "This is where I come into the story. I am a seer as well, but not nearly as powerful as Wolf is. I am what is called a healer and a channeler. I help channel the energy that bonding creates. I am sure you have felt what feels like electricity brushing over your skin. Like a shiver that keeps happening?" Bear asked.

"Yes Sir, I have," Gregory answered.

"Brethren Masters release an immense amount of residual sexual energy to the area around them, when bonding occurs. I help channel it so it is released in a way that doesn't hurt either the Master or the slave who is bonding. Without a release valve during bonding, the amount of energy that would pour through the slave could kill him." With these words, Gregory felt Bear's calloused fingers gently touch his leg. "So I step in, to help the process proceed safely."

The sexual energy poured through the room and flashes of light surrounded Master Wolf as he released his semen down his willing partner's throat. Bear seemed to ride the wave of energy, then turned away and addressed the two Brethren of the vision.

"There is a fourth here." Bear said. He seemed to not only ride the waves of sexual energy that emanated from Wolf, but also to straddle the worlds of the present with Gregory and the past with Mack and Wolf. What a remarkable gift this "channeler" had, Gregory thought to himself as the tattooed trucker brought the worlds of the past and present together.

The two Brethen of the vision, Wolf and Mack, turned to Bear in question.

Bear repeated, "There is a fourth here. There is a future presence here. A strong one."

Master Wolf turned, to see Gregory, although it seemed his vision of this future was dim and clouded. He frowned in concentration, staring in Gregory's direction.

"A 4th capable of many new things...wondrous things."

Bear and Wolf turned to look up at Gregory as Mack swallowed every last release from the Master's manhood.

The room dissolved around him, and Gregory and Bear were now standing on the porch, In front of them all sat Wolf, now grey-haired and naked, with several new tattoos and piercings. He sat quietly in a large chair watching the sun set behind the hills.

Finally, Wolf spoke softly and wistfully. "It was a good run, wasn't it, my loves?" Wolf turned to look up toward Bear and Gregory, then smiled. "I know everything isn't clear yet my new love, but there is a new life ahead of you now. I am simply at the end of mine."

Gregory looked down at him.

"He can't really see you, we are no longer in one of Wolf's visions, we are in one of mine...we are seeing Wolf's future... but he probably knows we are here," Bear said softly.

"You mean this is how Wolf dies?"

"Yes, this is his passing."

"I dont understand...how are we seeing Wolf's passing."

"it is so peaceful." Bear sighed.

"Good bye my slave, my bear...I rest well knowing our future is secure."

A single tear came down Wolf's cheek.

The energy flashed one last time and Gregory found himself back in the cabin. He was still in the same position between Wolf's legs. Wolf looked down at the human with great love. A pulse of the Master's sexual energy washed over them.

"I am your Master's Master, slave. Take my cock deep in your throat now, and bond with me."

Gregory reached greedily up to Wolf's cock. He began to swallow and take the cock down his throat, as he felt Mack's bare hand reaching towards his ass.

"Yes, mount your human slave, Mack. Take his other hole. Let us see his future together."

Gregory shuddered as Mack's large cock pierced his ass and buried itself inside him.

"Oh Master, it feels so good!" Mack gasped.

Wolf shuddered under the power of the bond that ripped through the three men. Bear could feel the energy begin to pour through them. He went to touch Gregory's leg to help focus the energy when Wolf took his hand. Bear was once again filled with Wolf's energy.

"No, not this time. Ride this bond with us, Bear."

A ripple of energy poured through their hand grasp and down through Bear's cock which engulfed his cub's throat. The energy poured its way through the cub's body and forced a wave of energy that forced the seed out of the human's cock.

"Master Wolf, this is different than before..." Bear yelled out

Bear pulsed once more as he released his seed down his slave's throat.

Gregory felt the energy ripple across his body. He could see hundreds of years of history passing through his mind. Master Wolf kept filling the human's throat with his cock. Bear then felt the wave coming. The surge of sexual energy like that he had never experienced. Blinding sexual need poured from Wolf, Gregory and Mack. The pulses of manly bonding flashing outward from Bear, through the very confines of the cabin and splashed over the Brethren outside. They could all feel the effect the waves of pleasures were having on the valley. Gregory looked up at Wolf and saw the pleasure in the man's eyes.

Wolf looked up at Mac, and grunted cryptically, "The slave

becomes the Master!"

Gregory felt both Masters, Master Wolf and Master MacElroy, release their seed into his body. It surged through him like a tidal wave. All three men rippled with the release. With the large dominant pulse of warmth and sexuality, Gregory's cock emptied for the second time all over the bed, coating anyone on it with streams of cum. Gregory could feel the wave of their love-making pouring outward. He could feel the slaves beside the bed receive the ripple across their skin and their minds filling with the need to release seed. He could hear their three unison sighs of release.

But for Gregory, it didn't stop there. He could feel the pulse of energy flow out over the valley. The orgasms and bonding that occurred outside of the cabin filled him with great tenderness. He had bonded; he would cherish these men forever, human or not. With that thought, he found himself falling into a soft, sweet darkness of contentment and devotion. All memories ceased visiting him and he fell into slumber, safe within the embrace of Wolf and MacElroy. Bear laid beside them with his cub soon falling into peaceful slumber.

The Wolf Clan slept.

EPILOGUE

It has been 20 years since I first found myself in the prairies of Kansas. My car never made it to Dallas, and neither did I. My home has been with Master Wolf and my MacElroy. I never called him Mack again after that incredible night of bonding. We would find out several things from that night: Master Wolf no longer had the ability to see into people's pasts and futures; that ability had been transferred to MacElroy through me. We still don't completely understand how—or why, for that matter. But now my beloved wears gloves with bright red "M"s on the sleeve.

At the age of 1000, Master Wolf once again began to age. He and his slaves have all gone grey in the temples, much to his absolute disgust. He is aging as gracefully as a dominant master of men can. He enjoys the company of the younger Brethren who stop by our little corner of the world, and regales them with tales of days long past.

Master MacElroy opened a Harley-Davidson dealership in Goodland. Surprisingly, it makes enough to keep both the dealership and the cafe going (even when we don't have customers at the cafe). I run the cafe now, under the careful tutelage of Master Wolf—although I haven't yet been able to make coffee to his satisfaction.

Master Bear and his cub have continued their trucker travels and have been all over the country. They return here for the cold winters and spend many an evening with us, making sure everyone is kept warm and intimate in the cold Kansas nights. They recently returned from San Francisco with the news that Patricia's nephew, Maximilian, has found a mate. Along with that news, however, came news that Patricia had passed away suddenly. Wolf took this hard, and spent several days alone that winter, contemplating the death of his old friend as well as the unexpected mating of her nephew.

The cafe flourished and continues to this day. I have celebrated my 38th birthday for the 20th time this evening. It seems that bonding has affected me in several ways. I find myself more in love with MacElroy and Wolf with every day that passes.

We are a simple little community along the interstate. If you find yourself in the need of a slice of pie, or a nice cup of coffee served by a congenial older man with a twinkle in his eye, this is the place to stop. If you know where to look, you'll find us, always here when you need us. So it's not actually "always open", at least not to everyone. You do need to know where to look and how to find it, and it really is only there when it needs to be. Chances are if you read this far, you'll find us right in the spot off I-70. Wolf's Cafe. Always ready to serve.

INTRODUCTION
CHAPTER ONE

He hadn't slept well. Tonight was no exception. He shuffled through the familiar darkness of his flat to the computer in the other room. The light was an uncomfortably brilliant as it invaded the quiet blackness of the room. Technology can sometimes truly suck. For Charles it was just another night of insomnia and unrest.

He wandered through websites that he normally passed through. The bear website had a couple of messages from friends, and one or two from new people. He browsed their profiles, not really finding anything of substance. He moved onto the Daddy website. It was one of those sites that rarely led to meeting someone, but at least the pictures were entertaining. As the pictures slowly flickered by in the early morning monitor light, he slowly became aroused. The new pictures soon ended and he flipped over to the leather website. The enjoyable, almost embraceable, silence was interrupted by the slow and deliberate tapping of the keyboard.

Leather websites always offered the best and the worst of the world beyond his simple flat. There were the men that were really into SM but seemed miles and miles away. There were those who were just on the site to tell their friends, 'you know I have a leather profile,' yet at the same time having real no idea at all what that meant. He had found some good people on the site however. There was the pipe smoker in San Francisco, the man with the ability to talk nasty in just the right vernacular to get him off every time, and some old friends who used this service to keep in contact with him as well. When you logged on at 3 a.m., you didn't bump into old friends. Most services allowed people to log in, and leave their profile available for view. but any message to them wouldn't actually reach them 'til morning light hours. No, at 3 a.m. on the west coast of the United States, you were lucky to find some Europeans entering mid morning, or Aussies horny after work.

Everywhere he looked there were no messages waiting for him. Typical. He took a quick glance through the people that had reviewed his profile when the one profile name caught his eye.

"SMOKEPROVIDER"

Intriguing. Pleasing to the tongue. He almost found himself saying the profile name aloud. It made him want to learn more. He tapped the Internet link and waited for his slow dial-up service to bring up the profile.

He walked away from the computer and to the fridge. A cold iced tea would solve the parchedness in his throat. He wasn't sleeping anyhow, what was a plastic bottle of tea going to do to him? Returning to the computer, the site had finally responded and the man found himself entranced.

There are times that you find yourself looking at a man that was completely your "type". The face staring back---no, the *body* facing him on the screen was something out of dark, nasty fantasies while jacking off before rest.

The man was in his 50's or 60's. There was a long, bushy, white beard that fell over his upper lip. There was a smile, but not wide enough to show teeth. There was a resilience in the eyes that made the naked man shudder just seeing them.

Charles Thompson could get lost in those eyes.

The gentleman on the screen was quite fit. A muscular chest, covered in a generous plume of grey hair, and two pierced nipples that shimmered with silver rings. Of course, Gregory could not escape the medium ringed cigar that allowed a small waft of smoke over the entire frame.

Charles smiled.

He slowly typed into the message screen: "Good Evening SIR. submitting my profile for your review."

He reached for the mouse to press send and paused for a

moment.

"Oh what the hell, he's probably asleep and no where near his computer. He doesn't even put a location in his profile, so he's probably in deepest eastern Europe." Charles sighed.

He pressed enter with his mouse and sent the message on its way.

He then noticed two attached pics on the profile. He clicked on the first pic to have a second smoke-filled picture greet his senses. This time the grey bearded man was dressed in a smartly tailored leather shirt and chaps. The cigar was still lit, and its smoke trail was still very present.

A grey jockstrap outlined what looked like a full crotch. Not escaping his eye was the outline of a large price albert piercing pressing against the cloth. It was large enough that he couldn't wear a jockstrap without revealing to everyone his jewelry. The type of crotch that he wished one could run into while working out at the gym. Just once, it wasnt asking that much was it?

He clicked on the second pic to find the normal "Must have owner of profile's permission to view this picture" block. He really had been hoping for a little more cock view. The guy probably wouldn't get his message for hours.

That was when the ding filled the room. He had a new message.

"SMOKEPROVIDER" one message, sent one minute ago.

He looked at the screen with apprehension.

"Oh he is awake and present, why not. respond. see what he said?" the man thought as he clicked the message.

"Good evening slave. that is what you are isnt it. I was actually just reviewing your profile and noticed what a good acquisition you might be. Just needing to be locked down and shown the warmth that a provider/MASTER can only give you...if still there, respond respectfully."

Oh fuck now what. he pressed reply.

"i am here, SIR," he typed back, and with a soft swallow he pressed "send".

He reduced everything else on the screen except the bearded

man's profile and the chat window. He couldn't help but be aroused by the whole proceeding. That a man who looked like that would even say hello. But of course, one could be using someone else's pictures. It was probably a unfurry, unbearded twinky in his 30s getting his jollies by teasing with his emotions.

A new message appeared in the inbox.

"Good slave. does it live alone?"

"YES SIR."

"Good slave, does it crave smoke? Piss? Flesh? Pain?"

"Yes SIR it does."

"Good...please log onto the normal chat program and add SMOKEPROVIDER to your buddies. we need to have a chat where we wont have any interuptions. You can give me the next hour or so boy? cant you...?"

"Yes SIR."

"Good boy, log on to the chat program and add me."

Charles turned to the chat program and immediately added SMOKEPROVIDER, and waited.

A single chat request window popped onto his screen and requested that SMOKEPROVIDER be added to his list. He clicked "Approve" and the chat window closed.

A second window then popped up, with the familiar picture from the leather service.

"Good boy. Log out of the leather site, this is the only chat you need right now."

Charles logged off the internet site.

"Good boy. Excellent in fact."

"Glad you approve SIR."

"I read your profile and determined you are worthy of MY attention. I look forward to having you...please me. and learn from me. and of course."

Charles waited for the last word in strange anticipation.

"Feed."

Charles couldn't really tell if it was the sudden addition of the air conditioning or the last word of the message, but he shivered.

"Feed SIR?"

"Oh yes, my sweat, my smoke, my piss, my seed. Not necessarily in that order either boy."

"i understand SIR."

"Oh you might have an inkling of what I mean, but to truly feed takes experience to take what I have to provide the right vessel."

Charles smiled.

'You like the idea of being my vessel, slave?"

Charles paused.

"Dont clam up on me now boy, answer."

"yes SIR i do."

"As expected. Now.just let me type and read. Don't respond. just read my words as they appear on your screen...understand me?"

"Yes SIR."

"Good Boy. I realize it is late, but I am pleased you find My schedule to contact ME. connected with you is pleasing to ME. I am pleased that I found you. true submissives are something rare. Let's just say I have a "sense" about these things."

Charles shuffled in his seat as he read the words. He was almost oblivious to the growing trail of precum on the end of his cock.

"I believe for every dominant there is at least one if not two or three submissives who that dominant is destined to interact with. W/we dont know if that submissive or Dominant that has appeared in our lives is the one W/we are truly meant to spend time with, or be intimate with. One can have many wonderful friends who fall into the category of Dominant and/or submissive but never really be true soul mates. But having kindred, or brethren if you will, is something that no one can take away from us."

Charles smiled.

"So, how do I know that you are someone that deems further investigation and interaction. I don't, but your simple reply and respect was a great pleasure. Most men on that leather site are just looking for jack off material. Your message was simple and focused. You greeted my profile with a great respect which I appreciated, and returned in kind, and you were led quietly to this simpler place to chat without interruption. Now, for inspection...turn your cam on."

Charles laughed into the darkness of his apartment.

"Dont keep me waiting boy."

Charles clicked on the camera and turned the desk lamp on so that the view would be clearer. He saw his well trimmed goatee and glasses come into the small camera window.

"There you are. just as handsome as the profile pics. I am assuming like a good boy should, you are naked. stand back from the camera, and turn around for me."

The man stood away from his desk as instructed and slowly turned around for the MASTER on the computer. He almost began to hear the hmmms and "thats good" "That's bad." coming in an imaginary voice from behind him as he turned around in full.

Charles found himself facing the camera and the screen once again.

"Yes, very nice. In need of some molding.but that comes in time. You would mold quite nicely I think into a treasured view. Just some ink, piercing and feeding. Long term feeding of course, of a special diet that only I can provide you."

Charles broke into a quiet grin.

"Ah I see you like that idea boy...good, its important to be willing especially at first."

Charles shifted in his stance.

"Sit boy. and now be prepared to answer many questions for me. I need you to interact without barriers," MASTER wrote.

Charles sat down quietly and tried to continue to look presentable into the camera.

"Good boy. Ready for questions? Just nod for Me, boy."

Charles quickly nodded yes.

"Excellent. 1. are you seeing someone currently?"

Charles responded no.

"Good to know. I dont fuck with other people's property, but I guarantee I fuck with my property in many ways. some it wouldn't even be aware of till the desired effect had already taken place."

Charles swallowed as he read.

"2. Do you live alone?"

Charles nodded yes.

"Good. pups with roomates just dont work. I need a slave that has his own space that is mine to invade at will, and also allow him escape into."

Charles smiled.

"Good boy...I like to see your reactions. That is encouraging. not to mention that hard drippy cock you proudly displayed. i liked that as well."

"Now, before I ask question #3, I need you to provide me an email."

"leatherinarizona@mailbox.com"

"Good boy, you will receive two emails from me. Open the first email only. Do not open the 2nd email till told to."

The familiar mail ding filled the silent air of the apartment.

"Fetch file one boy."

Charles did as he was told. The email came up.

"For your eyes only, boy," the email read and there was a picture attached.

The boy opened the picture to find himself staring up from the ground level at the MASTER he had been speaking to. There was a large fat uncut cock with a 0 gauge pa hanging out of the foreskin. There was muscular firm flesh surrounded by fine grey and black hair. There was the seemingly ever present cloud of cigar smoke in the picture. There were the eyes staring at him from above the cock, through the smoke and arousal.

"That is the MASTER who is talking to you now.slave."

Charles smiled.

"Gather that means you like what you see...its important."

Charles smiled with a broader smile.

He sat at his desk perplexed. He had experienced Internet come-ons before. The difference this time was, the messages weren't immediately heading towards sex. This MASTER/SIR/DADDY was different. He was investigative and invasive with his questions.

"Time to talk serious before we continue boy," MASTER wrote.

"As you had requested, no barriers SIR," Charles wrote back.

"HIV status."

"Negative SIR."

"I am as well. But regardless I would require new testing, and not to mention a measure of your resolve to be part of my life," MASTER wrote.

"Resolve SIR?"

"Committing to a relationship is simple to say, it is another to actually do so. My plans with a prospective piece of property is simple. You would submit, be drained of your seed, and locked up for 6 months. So when the testing happens I knew that your cock had remained mine for that entire period. To be truly intimate as I believe you wish to be. Once committed to a path it requires a resolve that many might not handle. If this continues to where we meet, you would be tested in many ways. Not just for HIV or physical condition. I'll test your mind and manners as well boy."

"I understand SIR."

"Thought you might (evil grin). Your daily interaction with me would become much more invasive. But, that doesnt bother you does it slave?" MASTER asked.

The comment took Charles by surprise.

"Not an easy answer is it, son?" the MASTER added.

"No Not Really." Charles said aloud.

"I dont read lips boy...no matter how handsome they are..."

"Sorry SIR...No. Your question isn't an easy one SIR."

"Take your time. I'll have your answer soon enough."

The submissive sat in front of the screen.

"No its not, but you already knew that."

Charles typed an answer, but then slowly erased his reply and began typing again.

"No SIR it isnt, but I know there really is only one answer."

"Continue slave," MASTER wrote.

"Invasiveness is what any true slaveboy would want, isnt it?"

"But I am not taking a poll slave, answer my question as I provided it to you."

"Yes SIR."

Charles took a moment to think out his honest answer to the Master's question.

"The slave would welcome invasiveness SIR."

"The only answer you are capable of giving, when being honest with yourself."

The chat window indicated there was more typing. It was always these points that left the boy nervous and excited. He knew more words were being typed. Were they bad words, or was the conversation going to come to an end.

"For now, leave my files that I have sent you, unopened. Don't worry I have set auto responses on them so I'll know if you sneak a peek. I require you back on this service at 1800 hours tomorrow my time. Do you know my timezone and the difference between us slave? for now on, all time references will be in my timezone not the slave's. Understand?"

"Yes SIR."

"1800 hours tomorrow then. be naked. have the camera ready. invite me to your camera and we will continue this chat."

"Yes SIR!"

"Dismissed."

CHAPTER TWO

It seemed like an eternity for 8 p.m. the following evening to come. No, not 8 p.m., 2000 hours, or 1800 hours MASTER TIME. He had found himself playing with his cock in the bathroom at work thinking about running home to a darkened apartment, and the hopes of interacting with this MASTER again. He turned on the chat service, and his camera. The Master's handle again showed on his screen. He invited the MASTER to view his camera and waited.

Several minutes went by and then his invitation for MASTER to view his camera was accepted. A chat window popped up.

"Good evening slave. Timeliness is next to my heart, thank you slave."

"Most welcome SIR."

"Now where were we. Ah yes. Locking you down for my pleasure."

Charles smiled.

"Good to see you can smile in the face of domination slave. I like a boy who can smile for me. For six months your cock will be locked down. Immersed in a device that will prevent arousal. It will be under my supervision (lock and key) at all times."

The slave swallowed reading the words.

"But. That isnt for a while yet. But know you have the choice of putting your cock in a lock in your future. If your future is with me, IT WILL HAPPEN. It is only a matter of when."

"Understood SIR."

"Yes, I think the slave knows exactly what is happening, and how far it would go to please its owner. That is why MASTER's cock is hard and drippy as I type to you, son."

"Glad you approve SIR."

"Now, as a proper introduction, you need to be aware. If it comes out of my cock, it goes into you. There is no negotiation here either. My Piss and Seed are for your flesh one way or another. Understand me slave?"

"Yes SIR." Charles could feel his body physically respond to the words appearing on the screen.

"We have covered my seed and piss, but there are other forms of invasion."

"Such as SIR?" Charles asked.

"What a wondrously inquisitive pig you are. Most would satisfied with my piss and seed. Your yearn to learn more is a nice trait."

There was a pause in the MASTER's typing again.

"Very well." The MASTER added.

A download screen came up on Charles's monitor.

"Download the file slave."

Charles clicked the proceed button and the file downloaded. A menu came up asking if he wished to open the file.

"This is the first of many files you'll receive from me. Watch it completely in your video viewer. Do not fast forward. Watch it all. and while you do, please keep the chat window and your camera accessible and activated."

"Yes SIR."

"When you are ready simply tell me when you pressing play, and I'll watch and monitor your reactions from here."

"Pressing Play SIR."

"Dont respond to my words that come up till the movie ends. Just read what I type and focus on the movie playing. Be a good boy."

Charles smiled into the camera as the movie file came up.

"INTRODUCTION ONE"

The title slowly dissipated and a voice filled the darkness of the room.

"So you need me in your life slave?"

The voice was deep and masculine.

"So you invite me and your introduction begins. Turn off all music, lights and remain naked as by now you are naked for me."

Charles reached to the desk light and turned it off. Only the television screen illuminated his office now.

"Good boy," the message window stated.

"Yes, you are a good boy. I mean my words. I don't use them lightly, slave," the voice in the movie said.

"As you know, I enjoy cigars. You will need to as well. As with liquids, so my smoke becomes part of your daily intake as well. There is no point arguing this point either. Invasion is all or nothing slave. Once you let me in, I take all avenues to feeding my property."

Charles grinned at that prospect.

"Close your eyes, and just listen to my voice now. You have me watching via your cam, and hearing the recording. I am watching you even now slave."

Charles could feel his cock straining to reach full erection. He closed his eyes and listened to MASTER's voice.

"Good boy. Any relationship with a MASTER and his slave begins here, in the darkness of introduction. The darkness of our mutual souls needing nourishment, needing the light that only a submissive and its owner can provide for each other. Now open your eyes upon your new light.

In the viewer was his new MASTER. He stood a ways from the camera. He had a skintight pair of leather jeans on, and lace up boots. He wore no shirt, revealing a furry chest Charles could bury himself in.

"Good to know you find me attractive, 'cause once I take you, I am the only man you'll even feed and have sex with. I don't share my property with anyone. Now maximize the video window so it fills your screen."

Thomas gazed at the MASTER's seemingly large bulge in the leather pants. The dark red amber that glowed in the man's beard entranced him. It was a medium sized cigar.

"You'll need my smoke. Just like you'll need my piss. These aren't occasional things that come from having a scene in the basement. Oh no. These are daily if not hourly occurrences. You'll be getting it whether or not you desire it. For now you just need an introduction to your future. Tell me aloud you need my smoke."

Charles swallowed but complied.

"I want your smoke SIR," the boy said out loud.

"Of course you do." the MASTER on the screen said.

MASTER stepped away from the camera and the sound of his footsteps filled the air. When he returned to the screen he had something in his hand. It was a gas mask. MASTER reached down to the camera and put the gas mask over the camera. Now MASTER's crotch was the only view out of the gas mask. There was no more full view. Two gloved hands reached to the zipper of the leather pants, unzipped and removed a fat large cock from underneath. The precum began to drip against the leatherclad legs.

"The mask smells like my smoke. You want my smoke, don't you slave?" MASTER asked.

"I want your smoke SIR," the boy said out loud.

"The straps won't let you get away, will they? If I feed you smoke, that is what you're getting, isn't it?"

"Yes SIR, it is."

The view of the MASTER was quickly glossed over by the invasion of smoke. It pulled to his eyes, which he immediately closed.

"Now keep those eyes closed, and enjoy my feeding, slave."

Charles could taste smoke. He could tell that more smoke poured into the mask.

"Don't worry slave. My smoke and my voice are all you need now, slave."

The woody scent of the smoke aroused him beyond measure.

"My voice. Listen to my voice and let my smoke do its job."

Charles smiled.

"You look comfortable slave. I have just started feeding however."

More smoke poured around the slave's face. Invasive was a good description of what was happening. He wanted to open his eyes and escape the smoke but found he couldn't.

"That's right, slave. There is no escape. Only your submission to me. And feeding on my gifts to you. Because in the end slave, your very breath will belong to me."

The smoke made the slave cough.

"You are still fighting it. Breathe with your MASTER's smoke slave."

Charles brought in controlled breaths and soon found the smoke mixing with his breath and becoming a warm friend in the darkness.

"That's it slave," MASTER's voice comforted.

The smoke slowly became something he wanted inside him. To take his MASTER's gift and embrace it within his body.

"Good boy, you'll also find this enjoyable, as I fuck you. And trust me, I will be fucking you as regularly as my smoke will fill your throat and lungs." A gloved hand wrapped around his hard dripping cock and the invasion of a thick headed cock taking the slave's furry ass in one swift movement.

Charles sat up in bed. He was greeting by the darkness of early morning. No mask. No cock in bed except his hard, drippy, morning hard-on. Sweat covered his body, and he could still taste the woody smoke on his tongue. The alarm clock on his bedside table read 5:30 a.m. No wait, that would be 0330 hours.

He lept from bed to his computer. A single picture of MASTER was on the screen. There was no movie file open. The picture was of the MASTER standing above the camera with a large cigar in his mouth. There was a gentle but knowing smile on the MASTER's face. Smoke filled the edges of the photo. There was a slave in the picture wrapped around the MASTER's feet with a smoke mask on. The MASTER was holding the breathing tube to the mask. Charles pulled up their chat window.

"slaveboy01: it would wear your mask proudly."

MASTER: someday you just might. But for now, it is time for sleep. Remember any emails I send you, don't open till told to. Just keep them in a safe place till requested. We will continue our chat tomorrow at 1900 hours. Good night slave."

The time stamp on the chat window was just after 2200.

The dream had been so real. He put his trust into the fact that it was a good dream. Charles turned away from the computer as the night's sweat dripped down his chest.

"Wow. Good dreaming."

Back at the computer, Charles didn't notice the camera was still on. On the other side the MASTER smiled. The slave had risen from his sleep. The slave's introduction was going well. He might have finally found a slave worthy of his feeding and attention. He had taken to smoke quite nicely. He took great joy in watching the slave get up from the screen earlier in the night and follow the video's last instruction. "Sleep well my slave. We'll continue tomorrow."

He watched from his chair as the slave showered off camera, brought a nice view of his furry ass in view as he passed by, and then dressed within view of the camera.

"Good boy," MASTER said softly. He then turned off his view of the camera.

CHAPTER THREE

One week had passed.

It had been two days since their last conversation and Charles began to wonder if the MASTER had lost interest. He found himself getting home and just sitting online waiting for the MASTER to arrive online.

At 11pm on the third night "SMOKEPROVIDER" appeared on his chat list.

"Good evening SIR good to see you."

11:15 p.m., still no response, but the MASTER had not logged out.

"Good evening SIR good to see you."

"I read your message the first time slave...doesnt seem very slave like to me, I think you are due for some new training."

"Yes SIR sorry SIR."

"Don't apologize. just turn your cam on, and fetch your email. more training needs to occur this evening."

The mail in beep filled the night air.

"OPEN and Proceed as before slave."

"YES SIR."

the slave opened the video file and pressed play.

"INTRODUCTION TWO"

"Good Boy...now enlarge the video screen full view. I'll be able to watch your reactions to the video to know if you are still interacting correctly.

You have done well to get to this point. but now some of my protocols must go in place...do you understand me slave?"

Charles knodded his head.

"Good boy.

First off, from now on you will ask permission to speak with ME when you see ME on line. you will "request permission to approach". Talking to me before you have permission is rude and inconsiderate on your part, understand me slave?"

Charles knodded in agreement again.

"We need to take your submission to me up several notches, and you want that dont you boy?"

Charles said outloud "yes MASTER."

"Ok then slave you know your rules when finding me online now, you are not the only person I interactive with online and sometimes, you'll have to wait your turn. Nothing turns me off than a pushy "talk to me, talk to me" slave."

Up to that point in the film viewer he had only heard his MASTER's voice. A single match light filled the darkness of the screen and it lit up the grey beard of the MASTER. The MASTER reached to the camera and took a hold of it. The camera was slowly lowered to the floor and then faced upward to the MASTER. The large uncut cock with its large piercing and all the body fur stood in the view. He looked down to the camera as he lit his pipe. The MASTER then reached to the desk lamp which illuminated a soft white light through the fresh layer of pipe smoke in the viewer.

"That is a view you better get used to. A slave within my reach is always right at my feet." the MASTER said.

Charles looked at the screen with almost guilty pleasure. This MASTER was a very handsome man.

"Now, we need to talk other protocols that need to enter your life. From this day forward you will send me a daily log of your activities; i.e. what you are doing, and what you wish for me to know. It should be sent to me upon your arrival home. Are you willing to do that for ME slave?"

Charles knodded in agreement to his task.

"Good boy, and I know sometimes it will simply be "went to

work, came home," but MASTER wants to know where you are. You are becoming something I wish to keep tabs on."

Charles smiled.

"You have every right to smile slave. not every slave who says hello to me on the leather site, gets this far. It is actually rare."

The MASTER paused long enough to produce another long cloud of pipe smoke down his chest and into the camera's lense. The lamp light seemed to dance...in the smoke and flesh in the camera's view.

"Now lets see about other ways you can please ME. we should start with saturday shavings. Starting this saturday you shall shave your crotch clean and send me photos of said work to show ME you are doing my request. This is not optional. It might take you a while to learn how to do it. But i trust in several weeks you'll be a professional at keeping my slave's crotch clean." the pipe smoking man said.

Charles swallowed hard. Had he heard the MASTER right?

"Yes, I said my slave. We are starting you down a road that few will travel. but you want this dont you slave?" the MASTER then stated.

Charles knodded yes.

"Good then. When was the last time you had a good intake of my smoke. We should remedy that."

Charles got lost in the smoke that filled his screen. For a fleeting moment he felt lost and insecure. It soon passed. MASTER was pleased. and there was more to learn.

FOUR WEEKS LATER:

The conversations in the evening time had become a nightly joy for the slave. The slave was becoming quite comfortable with the MASTER that had continued to enthrall him for the past several weeks. He had started sending a log to the MASTER daily of his appointments and things that effected the boy's day.

0700 Leave for work

0800 At work, plan on no overtime today. we have an appointment this evening. the slave likes being punctual

1600 the slave is heading home on the light rail.

1700 the slave had dinner with a colleague.

it has not released its seed within the last 24 hours as instructed, it is all still roiling in its balls SIR.

it is now home and ready for our interaction.MASTER," the email read.

The slave had pressed send. The sending of the log had become second nature to him. MASTER had wanted to know what his day was like. And if it strayed from the normal day of a slave, MASTER would then know what had been different. The MASTER was always careful to include things like "how was your day slave?" They often discussed the slave's feelings in situations good and bad. The slave was overly anxious to speak with MASTER this evening. There had been hints at a new mail this evening. He had been enjoying the others.

He was also enjoying the effect that interacting with this MASTER was having on him. Certain things that has strayed from his life were now returning. Every Saturday he was now shaving his crotch for this MASTER. Making sure that there was a picture of freshly shaved crotch in the MASTER's email box by 1200 hours, Pacific time.

Ah, the constant conversion of hours not only to military time but to Pacific time. There was no other time period for him now when conversing with the MASTER. He might live in the midwest, but it was the time on the clock in MASTER's study that gains his focus.

He had found that all his focus now turned to this man he hadn't met yet. It seemed like a good thing actually. There was a warmth and joy in making the MASTER happy.

"SMOKEPROVIDER" appeared on his buddy list.

"Good Evening SIR, permission to approach." the slave typed into his computer.

Then he waited. There were times where the MASTER would react immediately or maybe wait several minutes letting the sweat collect on the slave's head. There would be times where the MASTER would simply turn on his pc and toy with the slave. The slave knew that; but, that was for MASTER's joy.

"Good evening slave, approach," the response came quickly.

"Good evening SIR the slave's report has been sent, and the day was good."

"Good boy, if you were here...you would see the precum glistening from the tip of MY cock and dripped down MY pa."

Charles swallowed hard. How he had fantacized about being fed that zero gauge pa cock. There was a hunger there that he had never felt before. The slave wanted to bond with the flesh of the man who in just appearing as a screen handle on an internet chat service aroused him mentally and physically. He looked down at his freshly shaven genitals and was pleased at his own creation of precum.

"It is good to see YOU as well MASTER."

"Now, We have had some wonderful conversation over the past weeks, and I have been very appreciative of your attention and focus on MY pleasure."

Charles frowned. Here it comes. Rejection. The whole fantasy coming crashing down.

"But there will soon come a day where this will need to change."

The slave gasped. It was over that quickly.

"I have no intention of letting a slave as quality as you seem to be, get away from MY grasp. It is time for action." the MASTER typed.

An email appeared in his email box.

"Fetch your mail slave."

Charles rushed over to his mailbox and opened the email that MASTER had sent him. He also saw the second email that MASTER had sent him with a return email attached to it. He had been told not to open it till MASTER deemed it so. He skipped the mystery email and opened it promptly.

"slave, it is time for ME to come inspect my property. Do you agree with ME?"

That was all the email said. There was no dramatic wording. Just the simple facts. That was how the MASTER operated. There was no need for hampering a straightforward transaction between a dominant and a submissive wishing to gain more time with the dominant.

CHAPTER FOUR

"So, what are your thoughts of my email slave?" the MASTER asked back in the chat room.

"it is grateful and would be interested," the slave replied.

"I am pleased you feel that way because the time is soon at hand."

"It wants to please you MASTER."

"Good Boy. open the second photo, and dont log off after it. This conversation needs a proper ending, you promise me boy?"

Charles nodded as he opened the second email and sat almost dumbfounded. The view in the 2nd of the picture was of his front door. The glimmer of the desk lamp could be seen through the living room curtains. The timedate stamp was in the bottom right hand corner of the frame. It had been taken 2 minutes ago according to the stamp.

"You see.finding me wasn't coincidence slave...You were my vessel long before you found me on that site. You were mine long before you shaved your beard off to the goatee. And you will be mine.far after this conversation, but you knew that already didnt you?"

Charles nodded.

"Now be a good boy.and unlock your front door. walk to the center of your living room, and wait for me. Log off your chat boy."

Charles sat in a stunned silence.

"Don't make me wait boy."

Charles instintively turned the chat off, turned out the desk lamp, walked to the front door and unlocked the latches. He walked to the center of his living room floor, and dropped to his knees.

"What the hell am i doing?" he asked himself.

He then heard the start of steps up the concrete staircase that led up the side of his apartment. The steps continued in front of the living room curtain and stopped in front of his door.

"Oh god...," Charles whisppered.

The door knob turned and he could hear the door open. Charles didn't look up as the steps made their way into his apartment. The door closed. All four latches locked back up for the night. Charles didnt look up.

Two dusty boots then came into his vision as did the bottom of a dark black leather trenchcoat. The familiar scent of cigar smoke soon began to fill the room. He watched the smoke dance along the edges of the leather coat and then down to the boots.

"Good evening slave," the voice then said softly. A gentle older man's voice full of erotic energy.

"Good evening SIR."

"There will come a day soon that you might call me MASTER. but I know that isnt automatic, but that day will come."

Charles couldnt move. Then surprisingly the cigarman knelt and came into his vision. The endearing eyes filling his vision with a passion he had rarely seen in a man's face. The cigar was released from his lips and a large plume of smoke poured from his lips into the boy's face.

Charles, without thought, sucked in all the smoke he could.

"Good boy."

The man then stood back up and released the buttons of his jeans.

"Time to Feed my new slave."

The cigarman's uncut cock glistened with anticipatory precum.

Charles raised up and took the cock into his mouth. The PA slipped effortlessly down his throat and he soon found the entire cock down his throat. He worked hard to breathe around its girth.

"Thats it slave, take it all. Its all yours now, and as for you."

The master's hand grabbed the back of his head and thrust the cock even further down into his throat. Jason for a brief moment looked up at the cigar smoking man and saw the gentle smile in his face. The cock dove even further.

"Oh yes.even your breathe is mine now."

The cock invaded his throat relentlessly. Charles struggled and the firm grip of the cigarman wasn't letting him go anywhere.

"Don't resist me...let it happen. become mine."

The breath left his chest. The smoke invaded his lungs. The cock took one last plunge and the light of the world vanished. He fell into the darkness feeling two gloved hands holding him in place. Knowing that he would be safe no matter where those hands guided him, he continued to fall till the darkness until it was all he knew.

ASH
CHAPTER ONE

The alley was dark enough on an ordinary night, but fog had given it an ominous feeling. The dark folds of grey danced around the street light at the corner, blinding the passerby to the darkness beyond it. People went about their evening revelry in the darkness, oblivious of the actions beyond the light. Only someone in the alley would know the large clouds of cigar smoke mingled within the fog. The light only showed so much…

The man leaned against the brick building in the darkness in total satisfaction. His cigar choice was quite pleasing. He would have to remember this brand. The smoke also seemed to travel nicely from his mouth and nose. The cigarman loved how it clung to his body and traveled down to the other person in the alley. The cocksucker; a devoted one at that. This was someone that he would have to learn more about. For now however, he focused on the increasingly intense cock worship the boy was doing. The cigarman was pleased that the boy had shown no disagreement when told to kneel in the wet alley. No argument as the water on the pavement began to soak into his knees. There was even a glint of pure satisfaction...when the cigarman pulled out his cock, placed it against the boy's chest, and released four beers worth of piss. That ensured that the boy's knees were no longer something to be worried about.

The snaring of such a competent submissive had begun an hour ago, when Calvin had decided it was time to find a boy to empty his long-aching balls. Nothing really satisfied him more than lighting a cigar and feeding flesh to an eager mouth. He also knew that men of his appearance attracted many types of boys. The cigarman had the right to be choosy.

Calvin was 5'6", and covered head to toe with dark black fur. There are some who claim to have a treasure trail down their chest. The cigarman had many trails that led to many treasures. Some boys found all of them, while most only focused on the 9 inches of uncut cock between his legs. Actually when the boy entered the bar, Calvin already had an applicant on his knees, with instructions to massage Calvin's cock in its codpiece. The applicant was failing miserably. Calvin had leaned down and said, "Sorry, that isn't what I need this evening, boy."

The applicant simply got up and walked away.

No, "Thank you SIR!"

Some men just didn't have manners, trained or otherwise.

Calvin stepped to the rail and looked down on the new pup that had entered the bar. Shortly buzzed hair, a thick goatee, about 6', and obviously submissive; it all presented a nice package, a package that could be reformed into what Calvin needed. The boy ordered a drink and stepped into the back of the bar towards the stairs to the leather shop, which took up most of the second floor in the back of the bar.

Calvin made his way towards the leather shop. It couldn't hurt to see the boy in better light.

David hated the first part of being in the bar on Saturday Night. When you came off the street, you didn't smell of cigar smoke, you didn't have that bar scent. You smelled like automobiles and the fog. You smelled like the dampness that the night held for the revelers when last call was announced. He stepped to the bar and ordered water with a slice of lemon. David was also very horny and knew the rules. If he was going to spend a late night at the local sex club sucking cock and getting his throat ravaged, there would be no beer. If there was gagging it would simply be water. He liked it when men made him gag. Even better when he gagged, just to please the person he was servicing. It was all part of the service.

He had the feeling of being watched. As he made his way to the back of the bar, and under the overhang of the 2nd floor, he looked back through the smoke. Standing at the railing was a rare breed of man. There was hair coming from every follicle of his body, and the fine wisp of cigar smoke wandering his revealed fur, and tight-fitting jeans were an arousing combination. He had a tightly cut flattop of a dark black color. The cigar was not a large one, but it produced a nice amount of smoke.

"Piss first…," the boy said.

He walked to the bathroom in the back of the bar. He made his way past the pool table to the stalls of the bathroom. There were several handsome men in the pool area, but none seemed to measure up to the cigarman on the second floor.

He made it to the doorway of the bathroom, and quietly turned to look up the stairs to the floor above. The cigarman stood at the top of the stairs, cradling a beer bottle in his hand, and holding the cigar well within view.

David nodded quietly, and the cigarman nodded back.

"Got to piss…" David whispered under his breath.

He walked into the bathroom,went to the trough, slipped out his cock, and let out a great sigh as the flow started. He had needed to do that since he stepped on the train. The piss continued to spash against the porcelain as he continued to release.

"Impressive…" a deep voice stated.

David looked up to find the cigarman standing next to him.

"Excuse me SIR?" David asked.

"You can piss while aroused. Something to keep in mind…"

The cigarman came up next to him, and took out a large uncut cock.

"Is that water?" he asked as he pointed to David's water bottle.

"Yes, SIR."

The gloved hand of the cigarman reached for his water bottle and emptied it into the basin. He tapped the water bottle against the trough and let the lemon fall out. David watched almost in a trance as the man then placed the mouth of the water bottle over his piss slit.

David let out an audible gasp.

The cigarman soon started filling the water bottle with his piss, and the air around the two men with cigar smoke. David didn't really know how to react. The ability to piss while aroused had very quickly ceased. The boy just stood at the trough with an ever-hardening cock watching the bottle fill. The bottle filled and some piss flowed down the sides of the bottle.

"Good thing the next time you get to taste my piss, we wont have to worry about a bottle. Will we, boy?" the leatherman asked with a firm commanding tone.

"No SIR!" David answered firmly.

"Good boy. Now finish up with your cock, and join me upstairs. We have quite a bit to discuss before we leave."

"Yes, SIR!" David answered.

The cigarman then brought his glove, still holding the last drops of his piss, to David's mouth.

"Open!"

David obeyed.

"Suck!"

David obeyed.

"Open!"

The glove left his mouth, leaving David with an empty feeling until a large puff of cigar smoke then flowed from the cigarman's nose and mouth, wrapping itself around David.

"As said boy, finish up and come find me — and bring my piss; I expect it all drank in front of me."

"Yes, SIR!"

The cigarman then left the trough as he slid his hardening cock back into his codpiece. David looked in the cigarman's direction to find a thick band of leather caressing a very firm, furry ass.

David gasped once again.

The cigarman was then out of view. He fumbled with putting his cock back in his pants. He reached for the water bottle that was on the shelf above the trough. He took a deep breath.

With the piss-covered water bottle in hand, the boy walked towards the stairs and the cigarman at the top. The cigarman had said, "drink it in my presence…" He resisted the urge to gulp down the entire bottle right there in the bathroom.

He found his way up to the top of the stairs. The leather shop surrounded him, and he scanned the floor for the cigarman. He found him looking down into a display case. David walked over to him calmly, holding the bottle tightly.

The cigarman smiled.

"Good boy. For now, understand my name is Frank, but I am enjoying hearing you call me 'SIR'. It gets my cock hard, and that's your job: getting my cock hard."

"Understood, SIR!"

The cigarman smiled again.

"Now get to that bottle of my piss, boy!"

David tried not to seem to eager. The piss met his lips, and it was quite good. This man had his piss prepared for such an encounter. It was quite easy and actually enjoyable to drink.

"You like smoke, boy?" the cigarman answered.

"Well, like 'duh'," was the first thought to come out of David's mind. Not the best thing to say out loud, however.

"Very much, SIR."

The cigarman took the cue and grabbed the back of the boy's head. Soon their facial hair met as a great cloud of smoke was forced into the boy's mouth and down into his lungs. Every bone in David's body hardened. The touch of the glove on the back of his head was what took him over.

The cigarman pulled back.

"Excellent. Follow."

David followed the man out to the balcony overlooking the bar. There were several areas where the balcony fell back into slightly unlit areas. The cigarman stopped deep within one of these areas.

"Finish my piss, boy."

David finished off the bottle. As he released the bottle from his lips, the cigarman gave him another burst of smoke. This time however the cigar flavored tongue explored his eager mouth. Release.

"Kneel before me boy, and make love to my codpiece."

"Yes, SIR!"

David knelt without argument. He quickly starts outlining the cock within the codpiece. He could feel two large balls through the cloth that tightened at his approach and worship. Soon, a gloved hand reached to the back of his head, and pressed him harder against the leather.

"Show me your eagerness, pup," The voice from above commanded.

The worship went on for several minutes. The cigarman would randomly grind David's face hard into the codpiece. The boy was soon held in place with two gloved hands. He couldn't look up at the man. All he could do was serve. David let his mind focus on the codpiece and the man who filled it. It was all very pleasing for both of them.

The cigarman then grabbed him by an armpit and pulled him up. Just as he regained his footing, another blast of smoke into his lungs, and it left him dazed.

"Thank you, SIR," the boy said softly.

"You have my smoke and piss inside you now boy. You need to consider yourself mine for the night. You have this one chance now to walk away. If you don't leave, you are mine, cocksucker!"

David tried not to move a muscle.

"Excellent…"

A pair of Handcuffs were quite quickly placed around his wrists.

"Good boy, indeed. Nice to know these cuffs will get use after all. I have been carrying them in my coat for weeks. They were almost dusty."

The two leathermen made their way to the exit of the leather bar. They walked several blocks to the streetlight that the cigarman was all too familiar with. The cigarman led the boy through the brightness of the streetlight to the damp alley beyond, where he was then fed another lungful of smoke.

"On your knees, boy."

David obeyed.

The codpiece was unbuckled to reveal the full length of uncut cock.

"Like what you see, boy?" the cigarman asked.

"Yes SIR!"

The cigarman smiled as a fresh rain of piss poured down on David's chest. David began to move towards the pisstream.

"You take it in your mouth, and you don't stop drinking or sucking till I tell you otherwise," the cigarman stated.

David obeyed.

The cigar smoke seemed to billow out of the man's face at a greater pace, and it seemed as if it mixed with the fog around them. It seemed to envelop David and this cigarman in a veil of smoke.

David also felt something he had not felt for a long time. He had given true submission to this cigarman. To submit: the only thought as the cigarman's cock grew in his throat. He would gag, surely, as the cock grew. The gloves once again met the back of his head.

"Good boy…"

CHAPTER TWO

Waking to complete darkness was something he wasn't prepared for. When sleeping in his bed, there was always a hint of light coming around the blinds on the far wall. The room he found himself in was darkness itself. No slivers of light around a set of wooden blinds, no flicker of infomercials from a television left on hours before. It was complete and determined darkness. Waking soon led to certain other discoveries as well. He was bound to the pad on which he lay. The bindings were quite diligent in their role. Not only was he lost in darkness, he was beginning to enjoy it.

Then there was the matter of his cock. It was hard. He couldn't control it. Bondage did that. Not to mention it wasnt completely clear how he had gotten under the ropes. The memories of the night before his rest were not that clear. The events of the previous night were foggy, at best. A tinge of fear fell over him.

That was when the taste overtook his senses. His mouth was moist, but had a grittiness to it. It was like he had brushed his teeth with pumice. There was a fine grit all over his tongue and his teeth. If there had been light, one would have noticed the sudden realization in his eyes. The pumice-like substance was ash. Cigar ash.

A glow of a cigar. Of smoke. Of piercing eyes.

What had he got himself into?

He tried to move within the restraints to discover how much movement he had. He barely moved against the restraints.

"Ah, my ashtray is awake…" the voice whispered.

That voice. His cock dribbled with precum just hearing it.

"Yes, MASTER."

Master? He had never used that term before, why was he starting now?

"It needs to be fed, and then put back into rest. It will need its energy after the late night. Your training has just begun..." the voice calmly assured...

A dark grey beard harboring a large cigar. And the eyes. The eyes that stared with a sternness that he wasn't prepared for. The match danced with the end of the cigar bringing it back to life.

As his eyes adjusted to the total darkness there was a new light in the darkness. Much dimmer, but just as important to his eyesight; the burning embers of a cigar filled the darkness. The bobbing red ember came closer and closer.

A thick set of legs straddled his chest.

"My slave must be thirsty..."

As if thirst had been forgotten in the play of light and shadow, the captive agreed.

"Yes MASTER it is thirsty."

Who was this "it"? "It"—he never talked like that, normally.

"Well who am I to waste my piss on a urinal, when I have you?"

A large pierced cock found the opening to his mouth.

"Now, no spilling. We don't want a repeat of the first time, do we, slave?" the voice asked.

The captive's body suddenly remembered the bruising he felt on his back.

"No, MASTER."

"Drink!"

The warm flow of piss fell over the piercing and into his throat. The man in control let out verbal sighs as the flow increased to a stream, pouring down the captive's throat, with his gulping and gasping filling the silent room. The man in control let out a contented sigh as the stream lessened and finally left dribbles of MASTER piss on his P.A.

"Lick my piss hole, slave!"

There was no time for an answer. There was only time for compliance. The voice coming from the man over the captive made the slave hungry to please. Washing the Prince Albert piercing with his tongue was all he was concerned about.

The cock rose to the slave's attentions before being removed from his mouth.

"Good boy."

The ember blazed and then seemed to fade on the front of the cigar.

"Nothing like my warmth to wash your mouth out for its true calling..." the voice said softly.

The warm bundle of ash hit his mouth. At first he gasped. But, he found the more he tried to remove it, the deeper it covered his tongue and mouth. A dark, almost malevolent, chuckle came from the darkness.

"Good boy...take it all in."

He could feel the pierced cock that had once been in his throat hardening to a long firm length against his chest.

"You want more don't you, slave?" the voice asked calmly.

He wanted to say no, but "Yes, MASTER!" came from his lips and his mouth opened eagerly. It was rewarded with another bundle of warm ash.

"That is a good ashtray. You are going to be a good addition to my life," the voice said in its maddeningly calm manner.

Before he could think about it, the cock thrust forward into his mouth with a sudden burst of piss splashing against his face, some actually making it into his mouth.

"Ah. Knew there was a little more..."

The captive suddenly found his cock at full arousal, as the smell of fresh cigar ash and piss filled his nostrils.

Just as he had adapted to this, the ember floated up above him and the weight of his captor left his chest. He almost begged for the weight to return. It felt good to have his captor's weight holding him down against the relentless straps.

The ember went dim and a bundle of ash fell onto his chest, bursting out in a warmer burst of ember. Another load of ash fell on his chest, and with each successive bundle it was warmer.

He squirmed as the warm ash soon become hot ash. It would sting for an incredible rush of endorphin, then cool enough that the embers flowed over his chest in a rush.

He also noticed that each addition of ash more smoke filled the room.

"The slave is doing well..." The voice said.

"Thank you, MASTER."

"In fact, a treat before it returns to sleep."

He heard movement and watched the ember float above him.

The darkness gave him no warning as a very furry ass came into contact with his face.

"Eat your new owner's ass, boy! Do a good job, too—full tongue!"

The furry ass pounded into his face. He gagged when the air supply was cut off.

"I'll let you know when to breathe, slave! Now eat that fucking ass!"

He focused on the tongue work that was demanded of him. Just as he settled into a deep rimming of the ass that was presented to him, he felt the bundles of ash finding a new target. The throbbing cock of the captive was making for a good target for the falling embers of cigar ash.

"That's a good slave...eat Master's ass."

It was all the slave could think about.

Rimming ass, and going in deeper each time ash fell on his throbbing, thrashing slavemeat.

"That's it. Eat my fucking ass!"

The groans and gasps from his captor gave him great joy. He was pleasing his captor, his MASTER, his owner.

"Eat up slave!"

The man seemed to lower his ass even deeper into his face. Almost grinding the furry hole into the slave's hungry tongue. The smoke, the ash, the rimming all took the slave into a deep submission. It was a place in which he found great solace.

"Here is your reward, slavemeat."

The captor could feel a warm supply of cum pouring onto his chest. The white load splashing against his crotch, and with a single "Woof!" from the captor, the furry ass raised away from his face.

The darkness overtook him again.

The ember came down towards his face. Then he saw his captor.

The cigar dimly lighting the bearded face, and those eyes; eyes that before were stern were now full of joy and lust. The captor took a great draw on his cigar, and closed his mouth over his captive's mouth.

A large plume of smoke was forced down into the captive. He strained under the restraints, and the weight of the captor. His lungs burned as the smoke dove deep and took over his lungs.

The Master then released.

He stood back up into the darkness as the captive choked.

"There will come a day where you won't gag on my smoke. You'll beg for it. But soon you'll beg for everything I can feed you."

The ember moved away from him.

"Yes MASTER!" the captor said as he regained his breath.

"Only answer you got now, slavemeat."

The captive strained to see the ember. The darkness returned as the ember was quietly placed in an ashtray out of the captive's sight. The ember slowly dieing away, saving the rest of the cigar for the morning.

"Sleep, slave. Tomorrow we turn you over and start feeding that untrained ass my PA. You'll need your energy for that..."

The captive could hear the captor laying onto something.

"I said sleep, slavemeat. Don't make me come over there!"

With those words, the slave closed his eyes, dreaming of the coming day, and continuation of his training.

CHAPTER THREE

His dreams came to an abrupt halt. He opened his eyes tp the same darkness that had been there when he finally found himself able to sleep. He had no idea how many hours had gone by since then. Time seemed to have no meaning, when there was no daylight—or any other light, for that matter. There was a gentle sound in the air. He knew what it was immediately. Master was asleep somewhere in the darkness. Dreaming. Planning what was next for the captive.

There was part of the boy that wanted to thank the man for washing his mouth out of the ash, and letting him fall into sleep without grinding the ash in his teeth. Another repelled by the instance of his cock dripping with precum when the washing out was done by piss from a very sweaty cock. He had fallen asleep to the scent of that sweat that was ground into his beard as the man filled his throat with ash and piss. He was hardening even now, just at the thought of it.

How long had he been there? What was the intent of the man who had bound him? Was release going to be at morning? Was there going to be a morning?

Men just didn't disappear off the street into people's dungeons. The people at work would probably start wondering by Tuesday if he hadn't come in, right? Right?! There would be release.

He had noticed the bindings gave him enough movement to flex his muscles, and they didn't cut off circulation. Whoever the person was in the dark, he knew what he was doing. He had found himself in the company of a proficient practitioner of SM and leathersex.

Before he could react to that thought, he noticed the soft breathing across the room had stopped.

"What is it thinking?" the voice asked.

He was beckoned deep within to respond.

"That it feels relatively safe here… SIR."\

A single match lit the area to his left. It soon went out.

"Good. It is important that the slave understand: it wont always be like this, but it's important, for the next 24 hours, for you to be bound. You need to understand that taking my fluids will alter you…"

Many thoughts suddenly went through the captives mind. What the hell was this man talking about?

"You want more of my piss now, don't you?" the voice asked.

He fought it. Tell this fucker no. You don't need that piss. You really don't need that salty, wonderfully satisfying.....

"Yes Master, it does," he replied.

"Good answer, slave."

The heavy step of boots filled his ears.

"Open!"

The slave instinctively opened his mouth. He wanted the cock back in his mouth. Then the rain of piss fell on his beard. He quickly shut his eyes. His tongue reached for the salty piss falling in his face. Soon the stream found its target and the slave gulped up as much as he could; The remainder falling to his chest and pooling under his arms. His tongue searched his beard for more…needing more.

"That's a good boy: hunger for my piss. It will only encourage me to give you more. And by the end of this training session, you'll be well on your way to being my slaveboy. Addicted to much more than just piss."

The woodsy scent filled the air. This wasn't a cigar, but it was definitely smoke. Master stood above him, his dark black beard now dimly lit from a familiar device: a stonish washed white briar pipe. The burning tobacco within giving random bursts of life to his face. Letting the captive see his captor. The slave's cock hardened.

The captor knelt beside the bound captive and smiled.

"You see into my eyes now, slave. I like what I see. One of two ways to know you are pleasing me. Do you see my eyes in the pipe light?" the voice asked

"Yes Master."

The captor then took a deep long draw on his pipe. It seemed to take many seconds, and the slave knew what was coming. More Invasion. Smoke instead of ash. The man moved quickly and put his mouth over the slave's mouth. A gloved hand encasing his nose. All the smoke in his captor was about to go into him. No time for another breath as the smoke invaded his mouth and throat. Propelled forward by the force of the lungs pushing it into him. Tears formed. Tongues lashed at each other. The glove released. The Master's mouth passionately feeding and taking back the smoke they were sharing. Tears became passion.

The captive felt a warm glove on his balls. The hand then found his rock-hard cock. The tongue released from his mouth. Whispers of a beard against his ear.

"That will look good with my ring in it, slave, my piercing. So even at the gym, the right eye will know you are owned by another. You'll be owned by me, and everyone will know it. But you'll have to work hard for my three rings—oh yes, three!" the voice stated in a deep calm tone.

The captive struggled to get closer to the man.

"Ah yes. Strain against my bonds, slave. Let me help you with that," the voice taunted.

The ropes suddenly got tighter. All the relaxed movement he had gained during the night vanished.

"While you slept I went and got some things...open," the voice instructed.

The slave obeyed and a thin plastic tube was placed in his mouth.

"Suck!" the voice instructed.

His mouth soon filled with apple juice. He sighed inside.

"It's important to keep my slave in good health. I might go hard on you. And by the way, I have only begun to make that cock of yours hard with my dark room slave. Only just started. Don't stop sucking; drink it all, slave."

The Master moved away as the slave continued to do as told.

"You show great promise as a smoke slave, but I need more than just a smoke junkie. Oh don't misunderstand, slave. You'll be my smoke slave, but so much more. So today, we'll work on other sexual pleasures..."

The apple juice trickled and the sucking through a dry tube filled the air.

"Good boy. All done, I see," the voice continued.

The tube was removed from his mouth.

"I also took the liberty of seeing to certain things while you slept..."

The movement of the boots and shuffling of metal enticed him. A loud metal sound came down around him.

"Such a good boy..."

The two thick legs from the night before once again sat back down on the rimchair.

"As I said, you are going to be so much more for me than an ashtray."

On that statement the slave found himself confronted with a very furry asshole. The fresh scent of soap filled his nostrils. His captor was freshly clean.

"Eat your new Master's hole, son, while I take a look at the rest of you."

Two gloved hands took hold of his nipples. His tongue darted upward at the soft flesh within the furry ass presented to him.

"That's it. Show me how good you are with that long tongue of yours."

The pressure on his nipples continued. Soon the slave forgot about the worries of time, of work, or the world outside the darkness. Master needed his ass eaten. What else was there?

CHAPTER FOUR

There would have been times in his life if someone had said that by the age of 40 he would be tied up in a man's dungeon eating a red fur covered ass, he would have called them insane. But this wasn't an ordinary experience was it. This man knew how to get him to do things that he would never consider otherwise. He had always read in the magazines and handbooks that .it happened this way. This is what happened when you found the man who truly would reach in and find your true soul. He would nurture it.

This wasn't love. He had to keep telling himself that. After all. it had been a maximum of maybe 24 hours. He hadn't slept that long. In normal circumstances he wouldn't have been able to release himself to this man for such a long period. But he had mentioned during their initial conversation back in the bar, that it was the first weekend in a very long time that he had no plans.

The simple reply had made him tremble.

"Oh, you have plans now slave-boy. I will make them for you. You walk out that front door with me, and you are mine till i release you Sunday morning. Decide now...I am not one to tolerate indecision." the MASTER had said.

He had chosen to go with the man, and regardless of past inhibitions, he was eating the MASTER's ass. He found himself unable to stop. It was clean and sweaty. He also quickly learning the deeper and more thorough he worked his tongue in the MASTER's ass, the dominant keeper...would work his nipples hard through the gloved hands. and wipe the pre-cum off the top of his cock.

"That's it boy. get to know that hole, you'll be there often. Nothing better than putting a pup under my chair and feed him furry hole." the deep bass voice said amongst the moans of pleasure.

The slave loved hearing those noises. Those rare moments that the masculine nature of the man who was in control was released to let true emotion take over. Rare glimpses that let him know that pleasing HIM was occurring and being appreciated.

Then with a slight pat on the chest...the ass raised from his face. The boy's saliva coated his goatee in an animalistic type goo. It made him desperate for the ass to return to the chair. He let out a soft moan as the chair was lifted out from his frame.

"I see the boy enjoyed that as much as i did...good to know," the MASTER said with a joy in his voice.

A dim light filled the room. The slave turned to the wall on the far side of the room to see the MASTER turning a circular light switch.

"Oh, dont think light means you are getting out of my sight."

The light brought the MASTER that had confronted him in the bar back into vision. There was a tactile and visual aspect to the man's play that had the slave very aroused and wanting to experience more.

"We need lighten up for a while...I have the feeling you'll be back in the dungeon again quite soon. but we have other things to attend to now."

WIth those words the MASTER reached with his boot to a lever alongside the board and ropes the slave laid under. With a single click, the ropes loosened but the slave didn't move. That much he had learned. The MASTER came to him and knelt beside him. A semi hard drippy cock stood within reach. Again, the slave didnt move.

"Lets try to sit you up..." the MASTER commanded.

The slave tried to sit up and found himself a tad weak. As he trembled upwards, the caring hands of his keeper met his back. The MASTER reached again for the bottle of apple juice and handed it to him.

"Drink. Keep up fluids. We are going to get you into the shower, and then we are going out for some grub. You must be getting hungry, its near Noon."

"Yes SIR, food would be good."

The MASTER then stood up and looked down at his trainee. He had done well in the night hours, and he had found great solace in the slave's soft pulse of snoring when they slept. Frank Tosier had certainly found a wonderful specimen of slaveboy.

"Now, you get to experience one of my true pleasures with a boy."

The wide grin on the boy's face was encouraging. He extended his hand to the boy and told him to stand. The boy stood two to three inches shorter than his stance in boots. It was that perfect height for feeding sweaty pits to the boy...as he would soon learn.

He looked over the boy's body and smiled.

"Dont worry the marks the rope leaves will be gone before our shower is done."

"Yes SIR...no worries."

The MASTER took a gentle touch to the slave's chin and lifted his face up to his.

"You keep calling me SIR like that...and much more than your throat will be fed by this time tomorrow."

The boy just continued to smile.

"Off to the shower. follow me pup."

"Yes SIR."

They walked to the door of the dungeon space and into the house beyond it. They walked through the hallway. The boy was caught scanning his surroundings. The couple of men walked into the bedroom and there was audible gasp from the boy.

"Ah, you like that do you?"

The bed in the center of the room was made of thick wooden bars and had hooks in many places. The leather comforters and the sling laid upon them were quite a sight for those who hadn't been here before.

"Be good, and you'll know that sling well..." another brimming smile.

"YES SIR."

"But for now. to the shower...boots."

The slave didn't move.

"Remove my boots slave."

The boys attention quickly returned to him from the bed. A

quickly stated Yes SIR and the boy was all over his laces. The boots and the socks were quickly removed. The scent of a day and nights worth of sweat poured from his feet. The boy's hands quickly began to massage both feet.

"Massage later boy...shower ...first. Gloves."

The boy sprang from his knees and carefully removed the gloves from the Master's hands.

The two men walked into the bathroom and he then stepped into the large shower and started the water to pour down from the ceiling. He turned to the boy who stood quietly in the doorway of the walk in shower.

"Come on in boy, we dont want...water all over the house now do we."

The boy stepped into the shower and into his hands. The MASTER pulled the boy into his arms. Their bodies pressed together, as the boy shivered under the water. The warmth hadnt reached them yet and the water had a slight chill to it.

"Warmth is coming from many directions, pup."

The boy pressed in closer as the warm piss starting pouring out of the Master's cock. He could feel the boy want to kneel. He held on tight and then kissed the boy. There was a slight resistance, but soon the boy kissed him with intensity. Two cocks hardened below as he made slow deliberate love to the boy. He could still taste the ash in his mouth. Tasting his smoke and piss on his beard only made the cock arousal that much faster. The boy lowered himself to his chest and He cupped the slave's head in his hand. He guided him over to a nipple.

The boy certainly knew how to tend to a man's chest. His chest came alive with the gentle intensity the boy provided him. After proving the boy was apt, he raised up his right arm. The scent of a day's worth of sweat filled both of their nostrils. The boy lept into his pit as the firm grip led him there.

'Thats a good boy...get me all clean. Leave nothing for soap to render...eat that pit."

The now warm water poured down on them above. The leading of the boy's head ceased as he turned his head up into the falling water, letting the eager tongue and the warm steam rising around them relax him. This slave showed great promise, but there were many more tasks and hurdles ahead.

He wouldnt call it love. After all, the pup had only been with him 12 hours.

"So, young pup...?"

The boy backed out of the pit and stared with up at him with hungry eyes.

"Yes SIR."

"What do you like to be called. Your driver's license says Arthur. do you like Art, or Arthur?"

There was a slight initial shock that Frank had been through his wallet. It soon disappeared as they held each other under the water.

"Art.actually SIR." the boy said softly.

"Art it is...now.Art.you better get on your knees and take care of that hard cock...then we find breakfast..."

The boy dropped around his legs without another word. The warmth of the shower was soon joined by the warmth of the boy's throat around his cock. He cupped the slaveboy's head with both hands this time.

"Oh yes...swallow my cock boy. take it all."

He pressed slightly forward feeling a slight gag around his pierced cock, but the boy didnt stop. The warm slurping and worship continued.

Yes. the slave had promise. promise indeed.

THE GIFT

I arrived home at my normal 4:30 p.m.. One of the reasons I liked my job was that, although I did have to be there early in the morning, it gave me some quiet time at home before Daddy returned home. He has a christened name…but I like calling him Daddy or SIR whenever I can. He doesn't like me talking like that to him, 'cept in specific situations. One of those situations had surfaced. The answering machine had one simple message on it.

"First Message, left 4:29 p.m., May 19th Two thousand Four."

Then the slight pause.

"From 713-555-2284,"

Knowing that is Daddy's phone number at work makes my skin tremble. He left a message knowing I would be getting home any moment. He didn't want me to be home when the message was left. Knowing Daddy as I do, that meant something was up.

"Good Evening Boy…"

My name is alex. He rarely used Boy... accept when he is ready to play.

"Daddy, has had a really strenuous day at work. I am going to need some good TLC when I return home...to my boy. The dinner we discussed this morning, is sufficient, and should be in the oven. On warm. We might not get to it right away."

The sweat on the back of my neck tingles. "Tell me more SIR," I whisper into the empty apartment.

"Have a good beer, none of that cheap shit you buy when you go grocery shopping like an accountant. There is a six pack of Dos Eques Dark in the back of the fridge.....There is a fresh bottle of poppers in the

151

freezer. Leave two beers and the poppers in the small travel cooler on the table near my chair."

Daddy is in a good mood.

"You should find a plain paper sack in your closet on the floor…I want you to kneel on the floor of the bedroom and crawl to it. You will like what is inside my dear boy…and you will be wearing it shortly after I arrive home. Nothing else. Not even your favorite thick cock ring. Nothing else boy, understand? Don't shower either. You know how I hate it when you shower before Daddy is there to shower with you."

Sometimes I just do it.....to make him frustrated. My little secret (grin).

"And be ready for anything dear boy. leave the lube on the table by the cooler. I'll need it."

Daddy wants to fuck.

"I am going by the gym to workout. I shall be home round 6 p.m.. Be in the living room, in the item purchased, and be ready to feed."

The message clicked off.

My heart races when he purchases things for play. It is something he does very rarely. Daddy is practical. When he buys me gifts they are for our life, and my livelihood. I get dress shirts, and slacks so I make him proud at work. He never buys "play items". They mean special occasions, or simply Daddy has been really proud of me.

I walk down the hallway past the murals of photos of Daddy's family, and mine, and the one collage that is pictures of us. From the day I walked off a plane into his loving embrace, from the day I brought me and my teddies and he brought his simple but stylish belongings, the day we merged households in a new condiminium we called home.

I walk into the kitchen and fetch his beers from the fridge and the ice from the freezer. I find myself nervously fumbling under the counter...for the ice chest. I reach for the remote on the counter, and turn the cd player on.

The music fills the room. God how I loved this album. Daddy had left it on my many favorite songs. The specific voice makes my insides grove. Strange term yes. It makes my inside dance.

The cooler is where it belongs. My Daddy's beer is where it

belongs. Oh damn, I forgot the poppers. Its 5:30 p.m.. Can I wait…30 minutes for his touch.

Good. Found the poppers. Dad likes to give a big hit of them just before his cock plows home. It puts him in complete control of my hole.

I never used to look at my ass like that, before I met my Daddy. He loves to fuck. He called it … his hole. When he got pounding, sweat pouring off his brow as his cock burrowed deep into my hole. His sweat pouring down on me, and mixing with my own drippings. Our own special perfume.

I press the repeat button on the remote. I want this song playing when Daddy comes home. He'll turn it off. When he wants to. The remote will be up on his chair with the rest of them.

The song reaches a hauntingly beautiful orchestral climax. Silence. The Cd resets. The music slowly begins to climb through its soft introduction.

Time to go to our bedroom. To the place I loved being in at the end of the day. Nestled in his arms…caressing the man I love. The man I truly cherish. The music follows me through the house. God I love that technology…and Mom doesn't need to know that sometimes the music that fills my home is the music of sex and need, of hunger and dripping passion.

It would probably ruin several piece of music for my mother for the rest of her life.

Focus alex.

I found myself where Daddy told me to be. The message said kneel before the bed and crawl to my closet. Once on my knees I see the package clearly in the middle of my closet. One tight little red bow wrapped around the paper...put there by a man who normally doesn't show a romantic side unless provoked.

He was turning me on with wrapping. God I am in love.

I crawled as he asked to the closet. I opened it gently. I was going to use this bow again sometime. On a day where Daddy has earned special treatment.

I reached into the paper bag and pulled out the item. I smiled brightly.

It was a simple chrome length of chain and a lock. Attached to the keys within the lock, was a simple note attached.

"Don't put this on.....just put it on my chair. I know I said I wasn't comfortable with "collaring" you. I was wrong. I want it bad. I want it tonight. And you know as well I do, you will be wearing that chain under your tuxedo next week."

Oh that took me over the edge. I was hard...aroused...and happy.

Friday night I premiere in the new chorus that I sing with, now I live with Daddy. I am going to make him so proud. It is what I do. Feeling his chain around my neck. Oh god, how will I deal with that new set of emotions?

The song has repeated several times... i have lost track of time.

I break out of the emotions that the package created and notice the time on the bedside clock. 5:55 p.m.. Oh shit. He's almost home. When he says 6pm. He means the door will open promptly (sometimes I think he sits outside in his car…to time it just right).

As I walk towards his chair the music sings in my ear.

I turn the music down from "jamming in the house alone" to comfortable Daddy listening level. The chain and lock drop to the table beside his chair.

I sit in front of his chair...as I hear the garage door slide up.

He's home.

Oh god. The waiting is driving me nuts.

The door slams on the car. The garage door starts to slide down.

The knob on the door turns.

Daddy is home.

The door opens to reveal something I never considered. Daddy was wearing nothing but a full body harness and his boots. His cock was glistening with precum as it stood at full arousal.

"Daddy's home.....my boy."

He stepped through the door and smiled. In my head…I quietly sigh.

"Good evening SIR."

Daddy smiles.

"Ah thought you might find that CD ready for you..."

He chuckles. He walks up to me...his cock throbbing as he walks.

He reaches up to the remote on his chair and clicks several buttons.

My music vanishes.

Piano Concerto #5 Mozart. One of his favorites.

"It is a better day boy..." Daddy says with a smile.

"You get to suck Dad's cock for the whole first movement, pup."

I strain to reach his cock. He knows from the sitting position…I cannot move to reach it. Daddy straddles my body.....and drags his cock with precum dripping against my shortly buzzed head and settles in his chair.

"Turn around and greet my cock like my boy should."

I turn around. And get on all fours.

I take the head of his cock into my mouth. It throbs. It drips.

"Good Boy…now swallow like only my boy can..."

He grasps the back of my head and guides his Daddy cock deep into my throat. As my goatee comes in contract with his freshly shaved balls, I hear the chain as he lifts it from the chair. I know my throat shouldn't go anywhere. He drapes it over my neck and locks it. Then firmly grabs the back of my head. Burying his cock deep into my throat. Where he likes it.

"Thank you Boy... suck Daddy's cock... and make me happy like you always do."

I continue to swallow his cock as the first beer pops open.

He brushes the back of my head and rubs …knowing that turns me on more than one can describe. I am glad Daddy is home.

ABOUT THE AUTHOR

Drew McDiarmid lives in Houston, Texas, where he is a proud member of Bayou City Performing Arts, with both the Gay Men's Chorus of Houston and their small ensemble, VOCALEASE. Drew is 39 years old.

Drew has always had a passion for smoke, and S/M activities that can follow them. Drew spent most of the 90's involved with Orange Coast Leather Assembly in Santa Ana, CA. He also competed in the International Mr. Bootblack Contest at IML in 1997 and 1998, coming in third in 1997. He has also volunteered time with Leather Archives and Museum, and served as the Rocky Mountain Regional Coordinator.

Drew travels around the country to leather events showing the joys of bootblacking. He has shined boots from Folsom Street Fair in California, to Chicago's IML weekend and to the sunny shores of Florida.

Andrew McDiarmid is also the author of:
Smoke: Cigars and Men That Enjoy Them
Bootblacking 101: A Handbook

Available at Goodboner.com or your local Bookstore.